Writers notes:

Special thanks to my friend and biggest fan, Ryan Lewis for supporting me as a writer.

Credits:

Caolan McCormick, front cover artist.

Incendia

Ryan Kennedy pours a pint of Guinness into a branded pint glass with 'Guinness' labelled on the side of it in white letter markings. The handsome Ryan with his beard, long styled hair, gives a firm gaze at the pint glass with his blue eyes. He has that messy 'don't care about anything' look, yet somehow still appears neat and sharp at the same time.

Ryan Kennedy understands the importance of a well poured pint seeing as he is a keen drinker himself. That's how he came to be the pub manager in this place, a life of drinking and socialising here at the weekends. From drinking pints, to pouring pints, to managing others that pour pints; Ryan worked his way up the ladder over the course of ten years.

With his expertise, he pulls back the handle on the Guinness tap, stopping the steady flow of stout just in time before it overflows, then lets it settle for a moment. Ryan tops up the pint and serves it exactly how it should look, a layer of white foam on top, not too thick or too thin, exactly how it looks on the beer commercials or posters stuck up on the buses and tube stations. Brand perfection that only an experienced bar person could pull off.

It's a busy weekend here at O'Conner's pub. This is surprising compared to most weekends here – usually quiet! The busy atmosphere puts Ryan Kennedy in a good mood. It reminds him of the good old days when he was drinking in here when he was eighteen. This pub always seemed busy back then. Ryan came here to watch the Football. Back then you'd be lucky to even find a seat on a busy Saturday with several football matches on. These days however, things have changed, not for the better in Ryan's view. Those young ones are on their phones, their games consoles, sheltering somewhere watching Netflix on HD TV screens bigger than them in their parent's homes. It's clear no one wants to come out to drink anymore. No one has the money or interest for alcohol these days. The old lads had too many heart attacks or liver problems. The young ones don't care about Football anymore, or they care but can't afford a pint. Ryan can't help but feel aged already even though he is only thirty. It seems like everyone is so mundane and dead these days. What happened to a crowded pub with everyone shouting when a goal was scored? Year by year it seems like the crowds got smaller and smaller. At least today, there was a fair amount of people here to watch the Tottenham match.

Ryan Kennedy watches bits of the match while he gets a break from serving at the bar. He swears under his breath as Tottenham players slide and tackle, missing scoring opportunities. Being a Tottenham supporter is what first lured Ryan Kennedy into this pub in the first place. O'Conner's pub used to be a hotspot for Tottenham fans with everyone in the pub wearing those white shirts when those football matches were on. With Tottenham tattoos on his arms and back, it's unquestionable that Ryan was a devoted fan of Tottenham.

Serving at the bar isn't a requirement that Ryan has to fulfil, he's just doing it for old times sake. He's helping the two girls working behind the bar. There's a middle-aged lady with curly hair serving pints called, Maggie, accompanied by a cute young blonde girl serving alongside her. Ryan keeps the girls entertained during his shifts, mainly the young blonde girl who is called Christine. Not much has changed for Ryan in the girl's department. He still embraces a 'peter pan' style mentality for dating. Christine looks up to Ryan as the pub manager, making her easy prey. He already has her on the hook!

Ryan throws childish jokes at Christine all the time. "Why was the brain thrown out of the pub?", jokes Ryan to Christine. With a bright smile displaying her pearl white teeth, Christine giggles, "I don't know – why?", already anticipating a ridiculous answer.

"…because he was already out of his head", jokes Ryan. Christine laughs and turns away in defence of being lured by such foolishness, however the look on her face can not hide she's entertained. Ryan is only encouraged to continue grooming her while Maggie rolls her eyes at the predictable behaviour that she's seen a hundred times over from Ryan.

Two old men walk into the pub; retired firefighter Robert O'Brien and another overweight man known as Big Bill (no one knows Bill's real name). Both the men have the stereotypical look of the local pub goer; they both have beer bellies, and they both have tattoos on their arms.

Robert is bald with not a single hair on his head. Bill had short dark hair and wore black framed glasses.

"Alright lazy bollocks – let's give you some work to do, pour out some brandy!", jokes Robert to Ryan. Robert and Bill our lifetime friends of Ryan. The two men practically raised him in this pub – watched him grow up in a way.

Filling up a brandy glass with ice, Ryan reaches for a bottle of fine cognac from the bar unit, then pours a double into the glass. He gently places the brandy glass in front of Robert who sits down on a wooden bar stool followed by Bill who sits on the stool next to Robert. Ryan pours a pint of Fosters for Bill.

"Alright lads – keeping well I see", greets Maggie to the two men.

"Good evening to you love", politely replies Robert.

"You two fellas must be the only ones that still come here to drink", jokes Maggie.

"This is the only place round here that will still have us", humours Bill.

"Just about, I almost had to bar the both of you the way you were getting on last Saturday", jokes Ryan.

"That shithead dishing out all those sambuca shots until three in the morning, that fucking Bobby! I was gone before I knew it. You should bar that cunt instead", says Robert.

"Now don't you be blaming our Bobby now, I seen ya buying them awful Jaeger bombs, ya clown!", accuses Maggie.

"What? Me? Must have been some other bellend that looked like me. I can't stand Jaeger bombs", Robert defends himself with.

"I'll show the CCTV if you want, if ya dare to look at that", jokes Maggie.

"Those fucking cameras. They shouldn't be in a bloody pub", jokes Bill.

"They should like, to stop jokers like you two", says Ryan.

The two men continue to talk to Ryan at the bar while occasionally taking a glance at the HD TV screens inbuilt into the pub walls. Ryan takes a break from serving for a while and has a long chat with Robert and Bill. Christine serves the two men their next drinks. Robert looks at Christine without expression. When Christine heads to use the toilet and Maggie is busy changing the gas around the back, Robert freely expresses his views to Ryan with, "Bloody hell – look at her. She should be in a club on a Saturday night, not crammed in this shithole with your ugly mug".

Ryan smiles lightly in amusement to Robert's change in character. Robert is looking at the direction of the toilet corridor knowing that the young blonde goddess is in there alone. His face appears to display a mixture of pent-up feelings, like he isn't really sure what to do, stuck between lust and the law.

"Yep – she's a golden bar. The master deviant Ryan might have a date planned with her tonight", smugly announces Ryan to the two lads.

"Bollocks have you! What shite fairy tale have you told this one to get her out?", says Bill.

"Nothing like – I'm just being myself, do you know what I mean?", insists Ryan.

"What – being an utter cunt then?", taunts Robert.

Robert takes a swig from his pint, then desperately looks back in the direction of the toilets, his imagination filled with tantalizing fantasies.

"What would you do if you could get hold of that Robert?", teases Ryan in reference to Christine.

"It would be the first thing to hit the wall mate!", answers Robert.

Christine reappears from down the toilet corridor and Robert quickly returns his gaze to the HD TV screens. "Don't look, don't give her any attention", desperately instructs Robert to Bill, determined to not let his inner desires take his dignity. Christine heads back behind the bar and carries on with her work as usual, oblivious to the fact she's the topic of conversation.

Time goes by and more pints are served as the evening continues. Ryan finishes up his shift, Christine too. The pair of them put their jackets on and leave together. Maggie is left in charge of the pub for the rest of the night. Ryan smiles at Robert and Bill as he leaves with the young blonde gem, ready to take her for a night out. Robert looks back bitterly. "Enjoy your night lads. I'm out of this dump for one weekend", says Ryan as he puts his arm round Christine. She waves goodbye to Robert and Bill while smiling, dazzling them with her pearl white teeth.

Robert, holding his pint glass of beer close to his face (beer that feels like an ocean between him and Ryan) frowns slightly in bitter resentment to Ryan's success.

Before Ryan and Christine can set foot out the door, Robert abruptly yells out, "Oi", loud enough that everyone in the pub almost pays him attention. Ryan and Christine turn their heads back to him.

"You're still an ugly cunt!", insults Robert, one bitter last stand against Ryan before he escapes with that beautiful young girl.

Ryan smiles in victory and walks out.

Christine and Ryan wait at a bus stop a few meters away from the pub. The two of them are going for a romantic date into Harrow. O'Conner's pub (where Ryan works) is in South Harrow, the place he is standing in with Christine right now. There isn't much around in South Harrow. The whole area feels somewhat redundant with its international style shops hosting fruit stalls outside. The biggest highlight of the area is a fried chicken take-out shop located near the Underground station.

As Ryan and Christine wait for the bus, they engage in gossip, mainly fuelled by Christine. Then Ryan gives her the red-carpet treatment of compliments.

Ryan made no effort to break the illusion Christine had of the world. The pair of them step onto a red double-decker bus and sit down by the front windows on the top deck. The bus heads into town. A few stops and they arrive at Harrow-on-the-Hill, where all the restaurants and bars are.

Ryan spoils Christine at Nando's as the two of them sit down and indulge in food. The illusion continues for Christine that she's worth it all as Ryan plays to her own delusions. On the table in front of them is chicken wings, chicken legs, fries with chilli cheese powder on top, corn on cob, olives, and anything else Ryan could possibly order. Ignorant to Christine, Ryan perceives her as just another meal where she'll be discarded like the raw bone of an eaten chicken wing. Ryan will discard her the same way the waiting staff here at Nando's throw away leftovers on the plates. To Ryan, Christine is just another stupid girl for him to practice his drama skills. He'll pretend he's interested in the same thing as her. Ryan will even watch a whole series of the favourite T.V show that girl he is dating likes so he can have common ground with her. He will go through any length to maintain the act, all so that he can get his leg over for a few weeks, until he gets bored or finds a new girl to date instead.

The couple finish up their meal at Nando's where Ryan pays the bill. With his arm over Christine's shoulder, Ryan escorts her down the street in a gentlemanly fashion through the plaza between shopping malls at Harrow.

The next part of Ryan's master plan is to take Christine to see a movie at the cinema.

The couple enter the cinema. Ryan gets popcorn and other junk for them to share. By time Ryan is seated down in the cinema next to Christine, he feels restless and agitated. Suddenly, he's not interested in getting it on with Christine. He doesn't really want to be here in the cinema watching a movie he cares nothing about. "I'll be right back", whispers Ryan to Christine as he takes off from his seat and gently walks down the steps of the dark auditorium to the exit doors. Walking down the corridors outside the screens, Ryan follows the signs to the cinema toilets.

Ryan washes his hands in front of the toilet mirrors while running the tap by the sink. He splashes some water over his face to wash himself. Then he looks at his reflection in the mirror and is astonished how he's aged. The cinema toilets are empty leaving Ryan in a moment of undisturbed bliss. There is no sound at all. The only thing Ryan can hear is his own breathing. In this moment of divine peace Ryan smiles at his reflection having a decade of victory behind him. What does Ryan define as a decade of victory? A decade of women, drugs, and alcohol!

Just then Ryan's phone vibrates in his pocket. He lifts his phone out and holds it in front of his face. A message from an unknown telephone number appears on his phone screen. The message reads:

Did you think this was real?

Ryan feels shook up by the message and feels a deep sense of dread and regret. He knows in his head this reality is not right. He is suddenly aware of the terrible truth.

A pentagram forms out of cracks on one of the bathroom mirrors. It is a cruel reminder to Ryan that the fabric of reality is not as it should be. The pentagram is an evil reminder he is stuck in limbo, stuck in hell! There is no escape from this realm.

He backs away from the disturbing pentagram cracked in the bathroom mirror and rushes back out to the cinema corridor. Standing on that cinema carpet with the smell of popcorn, he thinks for a moment that it will be ok. He's lost his mind, nothing to worry about. The threat is all in his imagination. He promises himself he'll go get professional help as soon as this date is over.

However, Ryan's wishful thinking is discredited when the cinema doors to every screen open. Deformed ghouls flood out the auditoriums with rotten skin and glowing red eyes. It's a whole army of the undead, power walking out from every screen and marching down the corridor.

"Oh fuck me!", squeaks out Ryan in terror upon seeing the army of undead. He runs back into the toilets and locks himself in a cubicle. In this kind of emergency, Ryan needs something to take the edge off the terror. He lifts out a small folded up piece of paper containing a gram of cocaine. He then gently lines up the cocaine on the steel circular toilet roll holder hanging on the cubicle wall, straightening it out with his bank card. His eyes look to the floor where he notices the walking deformed feet of the undead ghouls lining up, visible through the gap between the cubicle door and toilet floor. He is surrounded! The next step Ryan takes is rolling a ten-pound note together until it is in the shape of a straw. Ryan uses the ten-pound note to sniff the cocaine off the toilet roll holder. His pupils dilate, he pounds his chest like Godzilla before roaring out, "C'mon then, you cunts, you fucking pale shitheads. You think you can take me? I'm fucking Ryan Kennedy".

Through the gap between the white tiled toilet flooring and wooden cubicle door is the sight of steel, gothic, high-heel shoes treading heavily, loudly, as they tap the floor with each step. The smooth skin of a woman's legs encased in purple fishnet tights is seen by Ryan. The sight of the demonic lady's steel high heels come to a stop and face him head on from the other side of the door, meaning certain doom.

Ryan stands up straight waving his clenched fists while bouncing on his toes in a boxing stance. "I'll have ya – ya fucking slag", shouts out Ryan. His words are cut short as the sharpest, shiniest, most solid steel shard (looking like a giant scalpel) pierces through the locked wooden cubicle door before then piercing through Ryan's skull and brain. Blood leaks out the front and back of his head where the shard pierces the bone of his skull. Ryan's eyes roll back has he passes away on the spot. The smooth shard is gently withdrawn back through the fine pierced hole in the wooden door. Ryan drops to the floor in a pool of blood leaked from his own head, bleeding out until the white tiled floor is soaked red. The gothic heels made of steel turn right as the pretty fishnet stocking covered legs walk away from the cubicle.

Chapter 1: All Alone

Fenton Wallace slowly unlocks the door to his flat in Camden Town. He's lived in this flat all his life. The scruffy looking Fenton has long hair the way a member of the band The Beatles would style their hair. It isn't a popular look. Fenton's hair looks like it hasn't been shampooed in a year. The skinny, scrawny looking Fenton steps into the dark flat he lives in. Fenton wears a grey hoodie that signals 'homeless' style look to anyone that sees it on him. The blue jeans he wears must be a year-old by now, they certainly look it. The jeans have rips and tears all over, mainly at the bottom where they've been dragged along the ground. The jeans are clearly too long for Fenton who is determined to wear them regardless. Fenton thinks these jeans are a cool grunge style look. Poor Fenton with his pale skin and skinny wrists, just another council estate rat, living on this council estate with his mad father, completely out of touch with reality. Richer and better-looking kids his age have conquered the world; they've travelled and had many different relationships by now. Not Fenton though! He's stuck in the mindset of a child, unable to progress or develop in life. He's eighteen years old, with no friends, no job, no girlfriend, and almost no family. Having no family at all might be a better thing for Fenton whose father is an alcoholic monster!

Fenton steps further into the creepy flat that is his home on the crime ridden council estate block. Junk mail and takeaway leaflets litter the floor by the entry. Fenton can smell the smoke from the cigarette that his dad is smoking. All that is visible from the sitting room ahead is a red light that shines brighter as the sound of inhaling is heard. The red light that is the end of a lit cigarette whizzes around like that of a fly. The monster himself, Fenton's father, is sitting in the dark smoking and drinking.

Fenton walks into the sitting room and switches on the light. The light bulb flickers on to reveal the rooms wallpaper faded colour from endless cigarette fumes. Cracks and dents are all over the cheap council estate walls. There in a worn-out looking chair is Fenton's father – wearing a white vest that is stained heavily. He sits there drinking scotch whiskey from a rocks glass placed on a small wooden table beside him. There's an ash tray on the table too. Fenton's alcoholic father with his grey hair and aged face looks up at Fenton while smoking on his cigarette.

"I don't it like it when you put that light on, we've talked about this Fenton…", says Fenton's father in his Irish accent. Fenton turns the light back out. The room returns to darkness as the tattered window blinds block out any light from the sitting room windows. All that is visible is the lit end of his dad's cigarette once again.

"Did you find a job yet?", asks Fenton's father in a croaky voice.
"No", gently answers Fenton.
"Then get out of my sight", abruptly demands his father.

Fenton walks into the flat kitchen that is crammed with unwashed dishes and mugs. Empty food packaging is scattered on the floor and kitchen work tops. The sink has limescale all over it. Fenton warms up the oven and places some turkey dinosaur shaped nuggets on a baking tray after taking them out of the kitchen freezer. While Fenton waits for them to heat up, he leans against the kitchen wall cupboards and work top. Outside the kitchen window are voices that can be heard from young men in the street below.

"My G", and "Are you mad?" or "my man is gassed", are some of the lines that Fenton overhears. That's how people his age in this neighbourhood talk, but Fenton can't relate. He just lives in his own bubble and keeps himself to himself. He doesn't hang around with the other boys on this council estate, the boys that are up to no good at all. Most of them are drug dealers.

Watching the oven impatiently, Fenton is desperate for the food to be cooked as he's starving. He only has £90 every two weeks to live on that he gets through benefits. Fenton daydreams about his lovely mother cooking in the kitchen like she used to years ago. She's dead now. He knows his mother is only a daydream now. She died of cancer years ago. That's what sent Fenton's dad off the rails, turning him into a mentally unwell alcoholic.

Bringing his oven cooked meal to his room, Fenton eats in peace far away from his abusive father. When he's finished his food, he then lays down in bed and puts some earphones over his head to listen to music.

All alone in the darkness of his room, Fenton drifts off into a dream like state with his eyes closed. He lets the music take him into the comfort of his own thoughts. The sound of his environment is drowned out. He imagines well enough that he is far away from where lives. He imagines he's in a desert landscape somewhere where it is bright and peaceful.

The sounds of smashing glass wakes Fenton up. It is morning now. Fenton's dad is screaming and shouting like a maniac. Without time to think, Fenton leaps out of bed and puts his shoes and jacket on. He leaves the house without getting washed or even brushing his teeth. He doesn't care where he goes as long as he is away from the disturbing behaviour of his dad.

There wasn't really anywhere to go. Fenton walks up Camden high street and admires pretty goth girls that walk past. He's attracted to the pretty girls in Camden Town with their piercings and tattoos. Poor Fenton hasn't had much success with girls or friends. In fact, he has no friends at all. He finds it hard to relate to anyone as everyone else he knew in London seemed to come from a stable background and monied families. Fenton had a small group of friends in Camden years ago, ones he went to primary school within this area. They lost interest in being his friend and grew more interested in music concerts and girlfriends. Fenton dismissed many social circles simply from feeling inadequate and unable to fit in. He was skinny and pale with a poor appearance.

Fenton decided he'll go to Harrow today. That's where he went to school. Fenton's mother thought it was a good idea to send him to school to a nicer area where there was less threat of him being bullied. Even though Fenton found Harrow to be accommodating and not as rough as the inner-city, he still made little in the way of friends. The young man was without social skills or confidence.

Sitting on the Metropolitan line, Fenton looks out the window to see Harrow Hill in the distance as the train he is on passes Wembley. The top of Harrow Hill is appealing to him as it feels like somewhere outside of London. The whole area is like a small town with traditional architecture and old-fashioned buildings. There was hardly ever anyone around the top of Harrow Hill.

Fenton walked out of the train station at Harrow on the Hill heading right towards the shopping malls. The poor loner would browse the shops just to pass the time. He knew he couldn't afford anything in the shop windows. He'd walk into electronics stores and check the prices for all the newest HD televisions. Fenton would even ask pretty girls about the products on sale, not that he was interested in them anyway. He just wanted to communicate with a woman. He'd often walk into shops and interact with the staff there. It was the only way for him to maintain his communication skills seeing as he didn't have regular contact from friends.

Come afternoon time, Fenton went to buy a fast-food meal in the shopping mall food courts. He'd sit there alone and miserable eating a burger and fries. The fizzy and sweet taste of cola that he sucked through the plastic straw in a paper cup comforted him. Food was one of the only things Fenton looked forward to in his day. Sitting there surrounded by tables and chairs, he listened to conversations from other people eating. There were all sorts of people eating here.

College students sat around a table eating fried chicken while yelling in slang at each other. There were parents with their kids eating around tables here. Sometimes there were young student couples talking about exam grades and their future career prospects over a burger meal. Fenton would always listen in. He'd let his food digest slowly while listening to the conversations of others around him in this food court. He'd have his head facing down with eyes looking at the ground, because he knew it would be creepy to watch people while he's listening to them. He disguises himself well. Now and again, he looks around to see the image of the people that he's listening to, whether it be behind him or to the side. It helps to put an image to the voice. Fenton sits here almost every day getting to know people without them even realizing it. Now he has an entire archive in his head of people and personalities. Fenton has studied the human population in secret all year, yet he still can't figure out a way to fit in with anyone. There just doesn't seem to be any common ground for Fenton to relate to people with. Out of hundreds of conversations Fenton has listened to secretly, he's hasn't once found anyone talking about anything interesting. He concludes he just wasn't made for this world.

Fenton locks himself in a cubicle in the shopping mall toilets. He takes a massive dump in the toilet bowl then flushes it away. Instead of leaving the toilet like any ordinary person would, he just stays seated for a while. It's comfortable and private here (although it smells bad). The shopping mall music playlist is playing from small speakers mounted to the toilet ceiling. Fenton just sits there for a good twenty-five minutes listening to disco classics. To Fenton this cubicle is a music entertainment booth. After wasting hours floating around the shopping mall, he heads up for a walk on Harrow Hill to waste more time doing nothing.

Fenton walked right to the top where the church stood with its tall spire that was visible from miles away. There Fenton sat alone wondering what went wrong with his life. There was nowhere to go and no one to see. It was dark now and the clear night sky with stars was visible. The red light on top of the church spire shined bright red. The roaring sound of engines followed by the sight of green and red lights in the sky jetted over the hill. It was a small plane flying to a nearby airport.

Fenton sat there on a bench in the eerily dark and quiet woodland surrounding the church. He was in no rush to be anywhere, least of all back home to that awful household he lived in. He sat there looking up at the stars, wishing upon them, begging them for a decent life with friends and a girlfriend. He looked at the stars and wondered about the far reaches of space. Was there anything out there for him? Anything here on earth or anywhere else way up there?

It was getting late now. Fenton knew he'd have to go back home eventually, so he got up off the bench and went for one last walk over Harrow Hill. He walked down a small road next to a pub where the street got narrow and parked cars were close to the pavement. A man approached from ahead…

Chapter 2: Friend

A young man the same age as Fenton comes staggering along the pavement drunk. He yells out, "when the spurs come rolling in…". Fenton instantly despairs this drunken yob on approach who wears a long trench coat. As the drunk approaches closer, Fenton deliberately looks down to the pavement as not to make eye-contact with the passing man. Just when he passed the drunken nuisance, Fenton hears, "Oi", from behind him. Do not look back, do not respond, Fenton tells himself as he carries on walking while suspicious of attack from the strange man.

"Don't ignore me, Fenton!", says the drunk. Then the shock of hearing his own name compels Fenton to immediately stop and turn back round to face the strange man that walked along this narrow road at such an odd hour.

"I'm sorry, do I know you?", politely asks Fenton who now faces the stranger. This drunk man looks familiar to Fenton as the sound of his voice seems recognizable too, but he can't figure out who exactly this person is – at least not in the dark.

"Like fuck you do! We went to school together for five years. It's me – it's Ryan – Ryan Kennedy", claims to be the drunk.

Of course – Ryan Kennedy, a good acquaintance of Fenton's from when he went to school. One could say they were almost friends in earlier years. After Fenton finished school, he went round for months handing out C.Vs to employers that never got back to him. He spent a whole year just walking the streets alone in isolation. It was a whole year just stuck in that dark flat with his crazy drunk dad. Fenton felt like a hundred years went by since he finished school. He forgot what Ryan even looked like. Fenton forgot almost everyone he went to school with. He looked in awe at Ryan Kennedy who somehow looked grown up beyond his years, completely changed in the one year since Fenton last saw him. There is an awkward silence for a moment.

"Oh, Ryan...hello man", nervously says Fenton who is deprived of any social skills. Another awkward pause passes by. Ryan examines Fenton while lagging on alcohol. Fenton's facial expression appears anxious as he feels like he's being judged by Ryan, leaving him unable to hold eye contact. Then suddenly the tall Ryan that looms over Fenton on the pavement in the dark, with his alcohol smelling breath, lets out a roar of laughter that is unmistakably mocking him.

"Well what the bloody hell are you doing wandering around Harrow at this time? I thought you lived in...Kilburn...no...Camden, right?", interrogates Ryan. Fenton feels embarrassed and exposed as the loner he pretends not to be. He knows Ryan is familiar enough with him to figure him out.

"You know, just going for a night-time walk. This is a nice area to be at", answers Fenton with the intimidation apparent in the quiet manner that he speaks.

"What? You're just walking around all by yourself at night?", calls out Ryan having figured out Fenton is most definitely alone. Fenton doesn't answer back. Instead he just smiles feeling like he wants to fall in a hole and die. It's humiliating to see a former classmate from school years looking down at him, as if they're not equal anymore. It used to be that Fenton felt normal, however, reality had hit him hard over where he stands in society the last year gone by.

"How have you been mate? It's good to see you. It's been ages. What have you been up to these days?", continues Ryan in a bid to get some conversation out of Fenton.

"Not much, not much – just looking for work and stuff. It's really hard to find a job right now", immediately conveys Fenton of his struggles in life.

"It sure is. It took me months before I found a job. I'm working in a pub down South Harrow. It's a good crack, good old place to work. Why don't you come for a pint with me? I'm heading to this pub at the end of the street. I've got an hour to kill.", invites Ryan.

Fenton goes quiet again. He feels like this is some kind of trick. No one is usually inclined to spend time with him on a social level as such. The presumption that Ryan wants to spend time with Fenton from merely a drunken moment registers in Fenton's thoughts.

Fenton is quick to dismiss the invite with, "Ah that's great, thanks. I'm broke at the moment with no job. I can't really afford to go out at the moment. Thank you though, Ryan. I better head off now mate".

"I'll buy you some drinks, don't worry about it. Yeah, come on – let's go for a pint. It's been ages", encourages Ryan with salesman like persuasion. Fenton is overwhelmed with emotion and shock. He never considered anyone would want to spend time with him.

Ryan was someone at school who he never had any problems with, unlike other kids that bullied him in the playground. The kids at school used pull his backpack off him and empty the whole contents onto the concrete playground floor. Poor Fenton would walk around collecting book by book while mean kids laughed and taunted him. None of these memories were attached to Ryan though. Fenton and Ryan never spoke much in school, however they had common ground having both gone to class in the same year group.

There was no other answer. Fenton felt too socially awkward and anxious to drink with Ryan, yet he also felt too awkward to say no. Without time to even think about it, Fenton said, "Uh yeah. Let's go for a quick one".

"That's it - good man. Here we go, here we go! It's going to be a good night", loudly cheers Ryan. The awkward scenario carries on as the two of them walk towards the nearest pub.

Ryan and Fenton set foot into a cosy looking pub at the top of Harrow Hill. Fenton is intrigued to go inside as he's walked past this pub many times but never had the courage to enter. It would feel awkward to enter a pub alone and sit there with no one. Now Fenton had a good excuse to come inside. The pub had vintage picture frames with old fashioned photos inside them all hung up over the fine shiny brown wooden walls. The bar display shelves behind the countertop were lit-up with bottles of spirits stacked up in an orderly display.

The usual pub noise could be heard; a mixture of different people all talking at once while the occasional tapping of pint glasses could be heard. This pub was full of people sitting on wooden stalls around square wooden tables. All the people drinking here looked rather posh. Ryan orders two pints at the bar where a pretty, young girl takes the order. The bar girl talks to Ryan as they know each other. They have a conversation with ease seeing as they both work in pubs. Fenton is envious of Ryan's social skills considering they are the same age and Fenton doesn't have the ability to talk to anyone.

Ryan carries two pints away from the bar and finds two stalls to sit on by a wooden table at the corner of the pub. Fenton sits down and takes swig of the pint in front of him. It feels gassy and bloating to Fenton, yet he makes his best effort to drink. Alcohol is something Fenton isn't too keen on, especially considering his dad is an alcoholic. His experience of alcohol is only tied to bad experiences. That was all about to change however…

"Ah fuck me – she's a fitty", confidently comments Ryan regarding the appearance of the girl serving at the bar. He takes a massive gulp of his pint having consumed one quarter of it already. Then his attention is undivided to Fenton who sits awkwardly opposite him in silence.

"Fenton…what about you? You seeing a bird these days?", asks Ryan.

"No", emotionlessly replies Fenton.

"Oh...are you working at the moment?", asks Ryan whose eyes direct back to the direction of the girl serving behind the bar.

"Erm...I think I told you already", awkwardly replies Fenton to the question about being unemployed. Ryan's eyes turn back to Fenton having realized he's not paying attention properly.

"Oh yeah, sorry, you said earlier. I'm sure you'll find something soon. You should do bar work like me. Anyway, how the hell have you been? What you been up to this whole year?", enthusiastically asks Ryan.

Fenton just takes a massive gulp of the pint in front of him. He can feel the alcohol getting to his head. Drinking didn't seem like a bad idea right now, anything to save him from the humiliation of a former classmate uncovering just how much of a failure he really is.

"Oh well, nothing really Ryan. I've just been looking for work and keeping my head down", says Fenton in a boring monotonal voice before taking another gulp of his pint. Another awkward silence follows. Fenton looks at the table unable to think of what to say.

Ryan realises quickly what he's dealing with - a recluse! It's evident that Fenton is behind on life in every aspect. Ryan can sense the lack of confidence from Fenton immediately. It's amazing how quickly Ryan can figure out the likelihood of Fenton's sad life. He also knows the struggles that Fenton has been through. Ryan recalls teachers telling him and other students to halt on the bullying when the school found out Fenton's mother died of cancer. Ryan knows the conversation won't come from

Fenton, therefore he takes command of the moment and dominates the conversation between the two of them.

"You have been through a lot...with your mother passing away and everything. How's your dad been doing? Is he alright?", asks Ryan while intent on creating a more accurate idea on how Fenton's life is going.

"Well...he's not doing the best at the moment", says Fenton while facing his head down in embarrassment of the situation. Further awkward silence follows. Ryan knows what he's dealing with now, he'd be sure to avoid any more sensitive topics for the rest of the evening. The same way a doctor analyses a patient before deciding the best method of treatment is the same why Ryan inspected Fenton. The perfect medication was right in front of them both. The famous pint! Ryan calculated that Fenton wouldn't turn down drinks he bought him out of fear of social rejection. Ryan would use this in his own favour and keep buying Fenton drink after drink. He thought Fenton should see what the pub is made for; to get out of your head and forget all your problems!

"I can't believe it's been a year since we were in that school. That bloody green uniform we had to wear, god! We looked like right tossers! Glad those days are behind us. Remember Mr Bukoo? He couldn't control the class for shit", reminisces Ryan.

This recounting of school memories instantly cheered up Fenton. The memories of the substitute teacher that could never control the students makes Fenton laugh.

"Mr Bukoo! What a clown that guy was. It used to be riot in his class. I remember paper balls being thrown around

like it was a battleground. What was it he used to say?",
tries to remember Fenton.
Before he can remember, Ryan catches on straight away
to the school-famous line that Mr Bukoo was made fun
out of for.

"Eh – stop throwing missiles", mimics Ryan in the foreign
accent that Mr Bukoo used to speak.

"That's it. 'Stop throwing missiles' is what he said all the
time when we were throwing paper all over the class. He
just stood there with his arms crossed with the hump", says
Fenton with an elevated pitch to his voice. Now the
conversation was flowing naturally. Fenton spoke loudly
and confidently. The alcohol was settling in as Ryan had
predicted.

"I don't know how we got away with half the things we
got away with in that school. Remember when Matthew
Jones threw that chair at Mr Foran's back? The poor
bastard was almost crippled. I think he was at home for a
week", remembers Ryan.

"Oh yeah", ecstatically confirms Fenton about the
memory in the classroom. He then bursts out laughing.
Fenton hasn't been this happy since forever. He's truly
over the moon now with the beers having taken away
any obstacles or anxiety that blocked his confidence
hours before. He's lost in the moment with Ryan, never
having been so grateful to have someone to talk to so
naturally.

"Was it you that beat Brian Hopper at Time Tripper 2 on
that new games console? What's his name? Mr Jones
brought in a burned copy of the game before it was even

out. We all got to play it. Didn't you beat that nerd Brian? You kicked his arse if I remember...", queries Ryan.

Fenton's face widens with excitement. He'd forgotten all about the day he beat Brian Hopper in front of the whole class on Time Tripper 2. Back then it was Fenton's favourite computer game to play. It was a first-person science fiction shooter that Fenton played everyday when he got home from school. Brian Hopper was a spoiled rich kid at school who played every game on every console because his parents could afford to buy it all for him. He was popular in the playground and was the go-to guy to talk to about computer games. One day Fenton got talking to Brian about Time Tripper 2 where he told Brian he completed the game on the hardest difficulty setting. Sadly, Brian dismissed the claim from Fenton stating that it's impossible. Then one day Fenton had his chance to prove himself in front of the whole class how talented he was at Time Tripper 2, where he did just that. He beat Brian on the game while the whole class watched the two play each other. Brian's reputation was toasted. Fenton felt brilliant that day, as if he were meant for greatness in life.

Sitting at the table with Ryan, Fenton smiles at the memory of Time Tripper 2 and the day he beat Brian Hopper at the game.

"You're right...you're right...I did. I beat Brian Hopper in front of the whole class", says Fenton with emotion. Both him and Ryan drink more beer. The two look at each other.

"That was a crazy game. Remember the characters you could play as? You could play as a fish. How mad was that?", delves Ryan deeper into memory.

"You could play as a fish on multiplayer. A fish…carrying a laser gun", jokes Fenton. Both him and Ryan laugh at the thought of a fish with a laser gun.

"Remember that level in the disco? I used to play as the fish and use the flamethrower. All that the other players would see on their screen was my fish character on the upper level shooting down flames onto the dancefloor", says Fenton so loudly he almost shouts it. The two of them burst into laughter so hard they can hardly contain themselves. The pair of them struggle to contain their laughter, laughing so hard that their ribs hurt. Neither of them could figure out if it were because they drank too much or just that they were plain stupid. They couldn't shake how funny the idea of a fish spewing flames from a flamethrower onto a disco dancefloor was.

The night has flown by where Fenton is drunk and has had the time of his life. It's only been a few hours and he already can't remember his sad life from before this moment. Just a few drinks with someone his age that he gets along with made the whole world alright again.

Ryan's phone rings and he lifts it out his pocket and places it against his ear to answer the call. A female voice so loud through the speaker talks, so loud that even Fenton can hear the voice from across the table. Ryan answers the call. Fenton feels like his bubble has been burst somewhat. Ryan has a girlfriend. Fenton listens to the call with fascination of the chemistry between Ryan and this unknown girl on the other end of phone. This alien concept of having a relationship with someone feels less alien-like and more real around Ryan, who proved a man could date a woman. Here was someone like him, with the same interests and age group, doing well in life. Fenton saw nothing but hope in the company of Ryan Kennedy.

"I will. No – I told you I'd be there at eleven, not ten…yeah…yeah…no. I'm coming now then, for goodness sake! Well, you know I like a drink out on a Friday night…ok…see ya later babe. I loooooove you", converses Ryan to his girlfriend on the phone before hanging up.

"You have a girlfriend?", asks Fenton, knowing the answer already.

"Yeah, if you can even call it that. She's a looker ain't she?", answers Ryan while holding his phone up to Fenton's face. A picture of Ryan smiling with his arm round a cute red-haired girl is displayed on the phone. For the briefest of moments, it felt like there was a knife being waved in front of Fenton's face instead of a phone. The photo was piercing and destroying as it was something that Fenton wanted so much. It seemed cruel in his mind that other people his age had relationships and he didn't. The phone is quickly withdrawn back into Ryan's pocket.

"It's been great to see you Fenton. You take care mate!", farewells Ryan as he departs swiftly. He slips on his trench coat as fast as possible and staggers out of the pub. Fenton is left alone with a pint in front of him, feeling awkward and out of place. His social phobia kicks in, so Fenton downs the pint and leaves the pub shortly thereafter.

Making his way down Harrow Hill to get the tube train home, Fenton suddenly has a rotten feeling in his stomach. He feels like he's spinning out of control. He leans over some bushes to the left of the pavement he walks on and vomits. Fenton can't handle alcohol. Once he's finished throwing up, he continues walking to the station. Once he's on board the train heading back home to Camden Town, he smiles while drunk, looking at lights lit-up in the night all over the areas the train passes. Fenton stares out the window with his mind joy ridden in happiness. He'd had something he hasn't ever had before…a good night out with a friend!

Chapter 3: Oddball

Another miserable day ensues for Fenton. He wakes up to his father fast asleep in that filthy looking armchair, the same chair his father is always sat on. Fenton was glad when his father was sleeping. This gave him time to get ready for the day in peace. Fenton has two slices of toast for breakfast, followed by a shower, before he then starts walking the streets again.

Yet again, Fenton is alone in the park on a bench counting how many ducks he sees swimming in the pond in front of him. Watching ducks is only entertaining for so long. While Fenton watches ducks dive under water and swim back up, he thinks how sad his life is. He relishes the thought of being back in the pub with Ryan; this idea soothes him.

The lonely Fenton wastes half his day watching the ducks. Sometimes he feels like his life is drifting away into a monotonous, slow vacuum of nothing. Adrift in daydreams and boredom, he is interrupted by the unexpected sound of his phone beeping from a notification…

It's a message from Ryan on social media. The whole world suddenly seemed like a brighter and happier place to Fenton. The suspicion that Ryan only spent time with him the other night out of being drunk was proved wrong. Indeed, Ryan wasn't talking drunken nonsense when he told Fenton he was glad to see him.

The message from Ryan is another invitation to a pub; this time a different one. Without question, Fenton immediately made his way to Harrow to what was surely going to be an exciting night.

It was night-time now. Fenton made his way over the notorious Harrow Hill that seemed devoid of all people. He was making his way to O'Conner's pub in South Harrow. This was the first time Fenton had ever been to this pub, let alone South Harrow. It was an area he never had any intentions of seeing.

After walking across the entire Harrow Hill, Fenton now made his way down to the other side by walking down a curvy road. The road was windy and twisty, passing large houses/mansions that were between trees and hedges, hardly visible until one walked past them. A frightening autumn breeze blew, rustling the tree branches and hedges. Fenton was creeped out. He always got nervous when going to new areas.

The creepy road down the hill soon came to an end. Fenton walked to his right for another five minutes down a long, quiet road. There was London Underground train tracks to his left behind a tall steel fence with barbed wire fitted over the top. The screeching sound of train wheels grinding the train tracks could be heard as an oncoming tube train approached. Flashes from electrical bursts between the train wheels and tracks lit up the area for a moment as it passed. The roaring sound of the train at South Harrow tube station was of fierce screeching as it came to a halt. There was South Harrow station, with the familiar circular red and blue London Underground sign mounted high above the station. Fenton was in the right place.

Walking down South Harrow, Fenton found himself to be incredibly disappointed by his surroundings. The first and most noticeable feature of the area was a chicken shop. It was a fast-food chicken shop with a silly name imitating the likes of K.F.C. Taking a quick glance through the shop window as Fenton walks past, he observes the interior. The staff are foreign, working hard as they are preparing burgers at the back while pouring chicken wings and fries into enormous friers. They all wear red shirts and white chef-like hats. The customers looked the very definition of urban youth, wearing hoodies, tracksuit bottoms, and trainers. Their visage looked criminal like. They appeared as the stereotypical unsavoury character you'd expect to find roaming the streets at night while up to no good. According to Fenton, the quality of a chicken shop in a neighbourhood determined the quality of the area itself. Finding a cheap chicken shop was a clear warning he was setting foot into a run-down, dilapidated area.

Exploring further into the depths of South Harrow proved to be disappointing for Fenton. Walking past strange off-licence shops that had fruit stands outside them, he thought how much of a dump the area was. The characters that walked past him in the street looked scruffy. The further he walked the more nervous Fenton felt. Why was Ryan inviting him for a drink in this slummy area? Was this a set up of some kind?

The nerves in Fenton geared up even more as he approached the pub to meet Ryan. There it was,

O'Conner's pub, all the way at the end of South Harrow. It was situated across the road from a curry house, next to a car repair garage. The windows outside the pub were glazed, making it difficult to see inside. A group of middle-aged men were gathered outside the pub smoking. They were all White British and could easily be stereotyped as your average football hooligan/The Sun reader. The men all had a big build physically, holding their bulging muscle pumped arms as they held lit cigarettes to their face for a smoke. They looked like brick layers or builders. For a moment Fenton hesitated to carry on into the pub. The thought to head back home crossed his mind, but he couldn't allow himself to return. His sorry fate was determined back home. There was only one hope, one way of life that could save him, which was the way of Ryan Kennedy.

Keeping his head down as not to make eye-contact with the men outside, he hurried into the pub. Upon stepping into O'Conner's, Fenton nearly had a nervous breakdown. The pub was packed with tough looking blokes in every seating area. Rough looking men were playing pool and yelling at each other at the far end of the pub. Fenton felt like a fly that just landed in a spider's web. He believed he was liable to get the shit kicked out of him at any moment by a drunken builder whose temper was short-fused.

"Fenton", is yelled from across the pub. His eyes widen sharply as Fenton turns to see who in the devil is summoning him by name. He was relieved to see it was Ryan Kennedy sat round a wooden table. However, Fenton wasn't relieved to see two huge blokes sat next to Ryan. The men looked mean and tough. One of them was a bald man that looked like he'd snap at any minute. The other man sat beside them was even bigger, who wore glasses, and had hands and arms so big he looked like he could crush someone's head like splitting a watermelon with his bare hands.

Ryan stands up and gives Fenton a hug. Then he says, "Fenton, my pal, thanks for coming. This is Robert", while gesturing a hand towards the bald man sitting down.

"Alright fella?", bluntly greets Robert while peering at Fenton. All Fenton does is smile and wave.

"This is Big Bill", introduces Ryan to the enormous bloke sat down next to Robert. Bill leans up and reaches out to shake hands with Fenton, saying, "Nice to meet ya".

Fenton shakes Bill's hand, as he does, he can't help but feel like a feeble mouse with his small hand gripping Bill's boulder like fingers.

"Sit down mate, have a seat, get comfortable", says Ryan as he moves up on the seating closer to Robert and Big Bill. Being comfortable was far from how Fenton felt.

Robert buys a round in for them all. Fenton finds himself downing as much of his pint as possible to try and halt his nerves.

"What team do you support Fenton?", asks Bill. There is an awkward silence followed. Bill and Robert focus their attention on Fenton, eager to get to know what kind of person he is.

"I...don't...support a team", mumbles Fenton.

Bill leans in over Ryan to better hear what Fenton is saying. He holds his hand in a circular motion around his ear to signify that he can't hear Fenton, then says, "say that again mate, I didn't hear ya".

"I don't support a football team", says Fenton loudly, almost too loudly. A couple of lads look in his direction as they sat on stools by the bar, eyeing Fenton with a look of disdain.

Big Bill laughs to himself and turns away from Fenton having deemed him unworthy of interaction already. Robert's face screws up, making him look uglier and meaner than he already does, which was bad enough in the first place.

Robert, frowning firmly, appeared like a rock golem that was unbreakable. He was fixed on Fenton the way a bull is fixed on a red flag before the charge. Then he questions Fenton with, "You don't like football? Are you gay?", rudely inquires Robert. Fenton sits there smiling while his cheeks turn bright red from embarrassment.

Ryan comes to Fenton's rescue with, "Look, Fenton here is different. He thinks in wonderful ways we'd never understand, isn't that right Fenton?".

Fenton nods in agreement with Ryan while still smiling like a clown and blushing from embarrassment. He drinks more of his pint, more than he can handle!

"What do you do for a living then?", interrogates Robert.

Fenton feels like he's been gutted from the inside out with a knife. Another humiliating question fired at him that felt like a canon ball hit him, seeing as he had no impressive answer.

"I'm looking for work at the moment", says Fenton who goes even more while bright red in the cheeks. Both Bill and Robert laugh at the answer. Quickly, Robert's facial expression turns back into that stone anger look.

"Where have you been looking? Under your own sofa? You live in London, fucking London, and you can't find a single job?", says Robert patronizingly.

Fenton felt like he wanted to sprint out the pub and down the street, however that somehow would feel more humiliating. Now he was so humiliated that his eyes started to water almost. He wanted to hide under the table.

Ryan attempts to rescue Fenton again with, "Now, now, don't be critical lads. It's tough for people our age. It ain't like when you lot could walk into a shop and get a job in the seventies".

Robert shakes his head in dissatisfaction to meeting Fenton. Bill seems equally uninterested. Another man, younger than Bill and Robert greets the lads. He shakes Fenton's hand to greet him as Ryan introduces the two. His name is Spiker. This man called Spiker has big arms, tattoos all over of them, and short black hair. Spiker immediately buys the lads a beer each. Now Fenton struggles to drink another pint as he is a lightweight. This bloke called Spiker sits down next to Fenton.

"Alright fella? What you doing hanging around with this nonce?", questions Spiker in regards to Fenton hanging around with Ryan. The reaction from Fenton was as awkward as could be.

Sitting there with a nervous smile, cheeks bright red, minor shakes, is Fenton about to go into a full nervous breakdown. Now there was four people he had to interact with, all of them strangers including Ryan. Fenton never really spent much time interacting with Ryan, leaving him almost a stranger to him in a way.

Spiker received a soppy reply that consisted of mumbling. A blatant lack of confidence is not respected by Spiker at all. Ryan, Robert, Bill, and Spiker enjoy some good old-fashioned banter as they relish their pints. The conversation between them is fluent and natural. All the while though, Fenton retreats to his own bubble and finds the group of lads intimidating. In a display of awkward body language and bizarre facial expressions, Fenton clearly expresses his anxiety and paranoia. In his thoughts he had hoped no one would notice him and that he'd remain invisible.

Spiker was agitated by the lack of engagement from this friend of Ryan's. He frowned as he spotted Fenton looking at the walls and ceiling.

"You alright over there mate?", asks Spiker. The rest of the lads at the table turn to notice Fenton's detached body language. Fenton blushes and smiles while licking his lips. He nods at Spiker to signal he's ok, then holds up the pint in front of him. The way Fenton holds his pint up to his face is like he's inspecting it, the same way a scientist examines specimen samples. Spiker's frown turns even more stern as he clocks onto the fact that Fenton is an oddball.

"Why do you keep smiling? What the fucks wrong with ya?", demands to know Spiker. The whole table of lads looked concerned.

"Calm down, who pulled your handle?", intervenes Ryan. Meanwhile, Fenton licks his lips in anxiety and strokes his hands together out of nerves.

"Where the fuck did you find this oddball? He's sitting there in the corner staring down the walls for the last hour", yells Spiker with a spiteful tone to his voice.

Bill and Robert laugh at the sight of the socially awkward Fenton coming under criticism from the intolerant Spiker. Ryan exchanges eye-contact with Spiker where he shakes his head in disapproval of the rude remarks towards Fenton. Doing himself no favours, Fenton looks into the direction of Spiker, still blushing bright red like a tomato and smiling like a clown. Then Fenton licks his lips nervously.

"Are you high? Are you on drugs?", abruptly asks Spiker. Fenton just laughs nervously at the question since he isn't sure how to react.

"Fuck me. Look at him – I've never seen anything like it", continues Spiker.

"That's enough for fuck sake. Leave him alone Spiker, I brought him here to have a good time", snaps Ryan.

The lads stop paying attention to Fenton. Ryan gets lost in conversation with Robert, Bill, and Spiker. Moments later a Tottenham match starts playing, where the majority of the crowd in the pub turn their heads to the T.V screens on the wall.

Time passes on through the evening as Fenton finally has some breathing space. The football match was the perfect diversion to allow Fenton to calm his nerves and recalculate his social strategy. He had time to recover from the lad's verbal blows. Fenton stared at the T.V screen on the pub wall like everyone else in the pub even though he didn't have a clue what was going on. He had no interest in football, he merely pretended to be entertained by the football match in order to fit in. The match went on with boos and cheers from people as players scored goals on both teams. Relentless yelling and swearing was heard throughout the pub each time a Tottenham player lost possession of the ball or missed a goal. Fenton used this time with everyone distracted to build his confidence in an emergency method; drinking as much as possible!

Fenton finished downing as much beer as he could, leaving him more confident for the next round of conversations. The match ended and the lads resumed talking. This time Fenton was loud and proud.

"How's that bird of yours doing Ryan?", asks Spiker.

"Which one?", answers Ryan. Spiker laughs at the answer in a genuine happiness to Ryan's answer.

"What about you in the corner? Where's your bird tonight?", is what Spiker asks Fenton.

Fenton, no longer embarrassed or blushing, confidently answers with, "I ain't got one. Not in a rush to get one either".

Spiker frowns and retorts with, "No bird? A young man with no bird?"

Fenton swings his head round and pulls a face like he's in a Jim Carrey film, then goes, "Noooooo sir, no bird".

"Have you ever had a bird? You haven't, have you?", figures out Spiker.

Fenton waves his arm and says, "sue me dickhead", before sticking his finger up at Spiker.

"Well fuck me! Where did that courage come from? That little cunt is sticking his finger up at you Spiker", comments Robert, pleased to see some chemistry developing.

"He'll be sticking it down the trash can trying to pick up his lost teeth after I've knocked them all out. Are you gay? Why ain't you got a bird?", carries on Spiker.

"He's a fucking woofter!", rudely taunts Robert. Meanwhile, Bill is smiling at the fire that Fenton is coming under from the lads.

"I don't need a bitch in my life. What's with all the questions? Are you gay? It seems like you can't keep your attention off me, mate!", counters Fenton. The lads laugh at the unexpected comeback from Fenton. Spiker is speechless, insulted, yet respects Fenton for sticking up for himself. The victory has come at high price for Fenton who quickly loses control of himself through alcohol.

The lads continue to chat. It's time for Fenton's round of pints.

"Whose round is it next?", loudly announces Bill while looking in Fenton's direction. He's expecting Fenton to buy the next round. Instead, Fenton just looks back at the lads expecting one of them to head to the bar and fetch him another pint.

Ryan lifts out a twenty pound from his pocket and stands up, ready to get the next round in. He hopes none of the lads are keeping track, but he knows better. Robert pulls him back down, says, "Hold on, hold on, sit down Ryan. I think it's someone else's turn to buy a round".

"I'll get it. He's broke and can't afford it", quickly says Ryan to resolve the issue.

"What the fucks he doing in a pub with no money?",
demands to know Bill.

"We came to an agreement. I told him I'd get the drinks.
Just leave it at that", says Ryan. Bill shakes his head and
clenches his fist out of frustration of knowing a freeloader
is in close range. For men like Bill it was tough growing up
and he was taught from young to go out into the world
and earn it, the same as Robert and Spiker. The lads
didn't take kindly to this stranger called Fenton sitting
there and taking beer after beer like it was on a conveyor
belt made just for him.

Ryan returns to the table with pints. Fenton necks down
the next pint. The conversation goes on and on between
the lads that talk about relationships and football, two
things Fenton knows nothing about. Dangerously so,
Fenton's head to starts to spin and everything looks blurry.
All the voices in the pub make Fenton feel claustrophobic
as drunks desperately try to talk amongst each other. He
feels invisible again like he doesn't exist. No one is listening
to him or paying attention. The lads beside him roar and
laugh in banter.

Desperate to be involved in the social circle, Fenton thinks
of the only funny thing that might impress the crowd. In his
drunken judgement, he recalls the last time he was out
with Ryan drinking and when they laughed about the fish
character spreading flames on the dance floor in the
computer game Time Tripper 2.

Fenton leans towards the lads and tells them, "Yeah, you
wanna hear this man, a fish waving a flamethrower over
the dancefloor. All the people trying to dance off the
flames on their backs...ha", followed by a laughing fit.

However, Fenton laughs alone. The lads are far from amused. Ryan feels embarrassed and awkward, wishing he didn't invite Fenton out.

Suddenly, Fenton doesn't feel too good. He stops laughing and stands up, swaying from side to side, eyes almost rolling back. Then he explodes vomit out his mouth, retching all over the table and into the lad's pints.

"Ooooooh for fuck sake", screams out Robert. All the lads stand up quickly and grab their jackets, vacating the seating area. Fenton sits down on a stall for a moment and the bar staff fetch him a glass of water. Ryan sits next to him and tries to talk to him. Half an hour later a taxi collects Fenton and takes him home.

Ryan is left helping clear up the mess. The whole pub smells like the inside of Fenton's stomach, forcing most people to cut their night short at O'conner's pub.

Spiker, Robert, and Bill discuss Fenton between each other, then lay it down to Ryan...

"That...is a fucking oddball if I've ever seen one. The way he just sat there and smiled to himself", says Robert.

"Look, he was just nervous, alright!", excuses Ryan.

"What kind of utter cunt comes to the pub without buying a single pint. I think you're being played for a mug Ryan", says Bill.

"He's a fucking woofter lightweight cunt! What the fuck you bringing him round here for? Where did you find this weirdo?", demands to know Spiker.

Ryan sighs in frustration before he fights back with, "I know him from school days, ok. You got to understand something here, my mate Fenton lives a hard life. His mother passed away a year ago and his dad is an alcoholic. It ain't been easy for him. He's a good lad, I'm just trying to show him something else other than the usual shit he has to put up with. I'd appreciate it if you lads just back me up here. Just respect what I'm doing".

"I'll keep my fucking thoughts to myself then", says Robert.

Spiker shakes his head in frustration. "Look at the chunks of vomit all over the place. He throws up in here ever again, I'll knock the cunt clean out. He's a piss taker!", says Spiker.

"He's a fucking muppet. If he's your mate that's fine. Don't expect me to buy his silly arse a pint!", firmly explains Bill.

Later, the lads leave the pub. Ryan goes home frustrated. For some reason he can't help but shake the feeling that Fenton needs his help. He knows that he can turn Fenton around from being an oddball. All it would take was some healthy social exposure and a bit of time. Ryan out of the kindness of his heart was determined to do it. With his head against his pillow before sleeping, Ryan thought up of some plans to help Fenton. This time he'd take him out again…but teach him some social skills first.

Chapter 4: Turning it around

Ryan is waiting in a café in Harrow reading the newspaper. He sits comfortably at a wooden table with an empty seat opposite. The staff behind the counter are frying eggs and cooking bacon. The café is almost empty. Fenton walks in wearing the same clothes he wore last week when he threw up in O'Conner's pub.

"Fenton my good friend, glad you made it. What do you want to eat mate? Breakfast is on me", invitingly announces Ryan.

Fenton smiles and sits down on the opposite side of the table. "I'll have a full English Ryan, thank you", says Fenton.

"Just don't throw any of it up", jokes Ryan. Fenton looks offended. Ryan folds his paper in half and gets up to order breakfast at the Café counter.

Later, breakfast is served and the two of them have conversation while eating egg, bacon, beans, hash browns, mushrooms, and toast. Ryan looks in disbelief at Fenton ripping up his food with his knife and fork, scoffing it down his throat like a scavenger. The way he ate his food was just like how Ryan imagined what dinosaurs would have eaten like thousands of years ago.

While the pair of them relax and have a cup of tea, Ryan looks around him to see the café still remans quiet. Both him and Fenton are in total privacy, where Ryan uses the opportunity to break some home truths to Fenton.

"We need to talk about the other night…", insists Ryan. Fenton's expression turns uneasy.

"Oh…I'm really sorry. I don't know what happened. The drink sent me totally out of control and before I knew…", tries to explain Fenton before Ryan interrupts him with, "It's not the throwing up that's the problem. It's…well, how do I explain this…"

There's an awkward pause and Fenton's eyes widen, and he breathes with his mouth open in tension leading to the upcoming criticism. Ryan takes a deep breath as he prepares to unintentionally hurt Fenton's feelings.

"What it is, right, is that you carry yourself in a really awkward way. You don't speak to people properly. It's like you don't know how to behave. When you told the lads about the fish in Timetrippers 2, well, they don't play computer games. They won't have a clue what you're on about. You see what I'm saying?", honestly explains Ryan.

Fenton pulls a worried face while looking Ryan in the eyes, but Ryan looks straight back with no mercy.

"I'm telling you this for your own good Fenton, you need to fix up. You come across as weirdo sometimes. You go red a lot too. Is that because your embarrassed?", questions Ryan out of curiosity.

Ironically, Fenton turns bright red while facing Ryan. Knowing that he's triggered some low feelings, Ryan switches the gears to positivity. He smiles at Fenton.

"Look, all you have to do is be confident in yourself. Don't take what the lads say too personally. Don't drink too much and throw up all over the place. What we're going to do, right, is go for another drink with the lads. This time I want you to ask them questions", instructs Ryan.

Fenton looks confused. He sips his tea and then answers Ryan with, "Ask them questions? Like what?", desperately asks Fenton.

"You don't know anything about them. Ask them what job they do. Ask them how long they've lived in South Harrow, anything mate. Get to know them. Honestly, I don't think you put yourself out there enough in mixing with other people. That is a very unhealthy thing. I know this is hard, I say it for your own good. I'm trying to help you out here", explains Ryan. Feeling uneasy having to give Fenton the third degree.

After thinking about it for a moment, Fenton agrees to Ryan's terms and conditions.

"There is one more thing…", brings up Ryan.

Fenton looks worried again before replying with, "Yeah…what's that?".

"We gotta get you some new clothes. You're dressed like you're straight outta the fucking nut ward", rudely remarks Ryan over Fenton's appearance.

Ryan takes Fenton into Harrow shopping centre and spends the day helping him pick out clothes, generous enough to buy them all for him. By the end of the day Fenton is dressed in jeans that aren't too baggy for him and a nice, neat top to match them. Even his hair has been cut making his appearance look neater. When

Ryan finally decides that Fenton isn't dressed like a complete nonce, he takes them back to towards South Harrow. He makes sure Fenton has a few drinks in a couple of pubs along the way before they make it to O'Conner's. Ryan figures a few J.D and cokes along the way will give Fenton just the right amount of confidence for when he enters O'Conner's a little later.

Come the dark hours after sunset, Ryan and Fenton stroll into O'Conner's pub looking sharp. They head over to the lads (seated in a different table this time). Fenton feels boosted by the moral support Ryan has given him today. The new clothes Fenton wears make him feel like a reinvented man (even though that isn't the case) giving him a confident edge.

Bill laughs at the sight of Fenton seeing as he can only perceive him as a clown. Robert shakes his head in disagreement with Ryan inviting Fenton back to O'Conner's pub. If It wasn't for Ryan being Fenton's friend, Robert would grip Fenton by the ear and drag him out the pub by it. Spiker is impressed by Fenton's change in appearance in which automatically gains some respect from him.

"Fuck me! You look like a totally different person. You're looking great", unexpectedly compliments Spiker.

"Oh, thanks Spiker. Would you like a pint?", asks Fenton immediately. This action is what Fenton was instructed to do by Ryan, loaded with a couple of twenty-pound notes Ryan let him have. The plan was to reverse the reputation that Fenton had already developed amongst the lads as being a bottom-feeder. Fenton was overwhelmed by Ryan's generosity, where he never really understood why he spent so much effort helping him. Nonetheless, Fenton was eternally grateful, and didn't want to question a good thing.

"Get me a pint of Fosters, cheers mate", requests Spiker. Through careful calculation and planning from Ryan, Fenton was able to effectively reverse the damage from his reputation.

Ryan and Fenton take a seat next to the lads with fresh pints in their hands.

"Alright you dopey wankers. What you doing? Wanking under this table all day? Good thing I'm here to get you lot entertained", says Ryan.

"What are you two dressed up for? You on a date with each other or something?", venomously speaks out Robert.

"Yeah – we're tag teaming your daughter at midnight tonight", instantly attacks back Ryan. You had to be sharp and quick in an argument with the lads at O'Conner's.

"We lost 2/1 last night. Wrong bloody odds again. Bring your magic back. You used to get the results every time. These days you don't get a single one right anymore. Next time I'll do the opposite of what turn out you say", complains Robert over football results and losing betting tickets from the betting shops.

"I'm working on it", answers back Ryan.

Robert takes a look at Fenton and frowns.

"You got some iron pair on ya to be coming back in here after last time. Should you be drinking that? I can get a bottle of milk for ya instead. Save ya throwing up all over the gaff. This carpet still smells of your stomach", insultingly remarks Robert to Fenton.

Fenton laughs, he laughs Robert's remark away. That was one of the most difficult yet best moments of his life. For the first time he took the insult on the chest and deflected it like he was made of steel. For the first time ever, Fenton let go of the worries of what people thought about him, because he knew it truly didn't matter. After he laughed there was nothing more to say about it. Robert could only move on and talk about something else as time transported the awkward moment away. Fenton felt indestructible.

The lads talked away where Fenton let himself go in the moment. He started talking to Big Bill who seemed the quietest and most reserved.

"So Big Bill...how long have you lived in South Harrow?", asks Fenton in order to get some conversation going.

"All my life", answers Bill. "Where do you live?", Bill asks Fenton.

"I live in Camden Town", answers Fenton.

"Camden? What you doing all the way here then?", eagerly asks Bill in astonishment.

"I prefer it in Harrow. This is a nice area", lies Fenton. The real answer is that he's here because this is the only social circle that's been tolerant of him. Hanging out in Harrow was his only choice. If Fenton could, he would be hanging out with pretty, inner-city girls, where there was plenty of them walking the streets in Camden Town. Instead, he was here in a pub with men twice his age.

"What do you do for a living?", asks Fenton to find out what job Bill has.

"I am an engineer for the London Underground", says Bill.

"That's…that sounds hard. What do you have to do for that?", asks Fenton with interest.

"I walk up and down those train tracks at night taking them apart and putting them back together again while your tucked in bed sleeping and dreaming of sheep", replies Bill.

There is a mutual silence and Fenton takes a gulp of his pint.

"What are you doing at the moment? Nothing!", asks Bill while already providing the answer to his own question. Fenton nods in confirmation of the answer. Bill lets out a mocking laugh.

"I used to go in and take trains apart at your age. Not being funny, get a job mate! You gotta have a job", states Bill.

Fenton stops talking to Bill for the time being. Miraculously, Spiker comes to Fenton's rescue with an upbeat attitude.

"Fenton, I heard about your situation at home and losing your mum. It sounds like a shit life! That's life though, it takes a knock-out punch at ya now and again. The most important thing is that you keep yourself going. Ya know what I mean?", says Spiker.

"I know what you mean", briefly returns Fenton before asking Spiker, "You lived in South Harrow all your life?".

"Most of my life. I come from Essex. I moved to South Harrow in the eighties. This area was a really good area back then. I don't know what's happened to it now though. All these foreigners have come over here and turned it into a shithole", rants Spiker.

"It's not the best area in the world. What do you do for a living?", continues Fenton.

"I'm a lorry driver", answers Spiker.

"How long you been doing that for?", questions Fenton.

"Fuck me – for as long as I can remember. I worked in the butchers before that. I been working all my life. I'm a slave to money. It's alright though. I got money to spend on my birds, ya know what I mean?", says Spiker.

"I hope to be like you one day with a good job and bird", comments Fenton.

Spiker's facial expression turns more serious. Fenton looks at him with realisation that thoughts are whirling around in Spiker's mind.

"I'm sorry…I thought…so you're not that way after all?", says Spiker.

"Not what?", desperately asks Fenton in confusion about what Spiker is talking about.

"I really thought you were, ya know, a member of the gay community", explains Spiker.

Fenton feels insulted and humiliated which causes his facial expression to turn firm. For the first time in the night, he turns bright red in embarrassment. Awkward silence follows where Spiker looks into Fenton's eyes with solid faith in what he believes. It feels to Fenton that Spiker is waiting for him to say something…

"It's alright if your gay Fenton. No one here cares like, do you know what I mean mate? You can express yourself around here", comfortingly explains Spiker.

Fenton feels furious inside. He uses all his focus and discipline in order to not erupt into shouting and arguing.

"That's nice of you Spiker. I'm not gay. There's no need to worry about that", says Fenton as reassuringly as he can while letting out a forced laugh, trying to convey that the idea of him being perceived as gay is ludicrous.

Spiker puts his arm on Fenton's shoulder to comfort him, attempts to provoke Fenton to 'come out of the closet' one last time with, "That's good to hear mate. If you ever was gay, I'd like you to know you'd never to worry about that around us in this pub".

Spiker nods at Fenton to confirm the seriousness of what he's saying as he removes his hand from Fenton's shoulder. Never in his whole life has Fenton felt so close to erupting. Like a volcano, Fenton just wanted to get up and roar out to the whole pub, 'I AM NOT GAY!". He didn't though. He couldn't! Reacting like that would make it look like he was angry and confused by his sexuality. Instead, Fenton just took a deep breath and focused on finishing his pint.

Finally, Fenton got a moment with Robert. This was more difficult as Robert had the least amount of respect for Fenton.

"Oh, hiya Robert. How's it going? What's up?", asks Fenton. Robert frowns in return to the question and doesn't answer it for a moment. "Fuck me, look who it is. Don't come too close to me mate. I don't want you throwing up all over my trousers", warns Robert.

Fenton just smiles and sits next to Robert who stares him down. "What are you smiling at? You been smoking dope or something?", asks Robert. In turn this makes Fenton smile more as he's nervous. Robert laughs at Fenton believing he's a clown. Fenton won't let being laughed at by Robert get to his head, so he takes a seat casually next to Robert.

"How long you been living in South Harrow, Robert?", asks Fenton.

"Since before your silly bollocks was conceived", bluntly answers Robert.

"What do you do for a living?", enquires Fenton.

"I'm a retired firefighter. I spent thirty-six years putting out flames. I've watched people's homes go up in blazes, then seen people break down on their knees in tears because they've lost everything they own. I've seen it all mate. What about you? A young man like you must be hard at work? You found a job yet?", Robert turns the conversation around with.

"I'm looking for work. I ain't found anything yet", says Fenton. Robert shakes his head in disapproval before gunning back with, "What do you do all day then? Sit around wanking? Please tell me you've at least got a bird to spend time with?".

"I don't have a girlfriend; I dated a couple of birds last year. Right now, I have no one", hesitantly answers Fenton. Robert screams out laughing in hysterics. Fenton struggles to figure out what Robert finds so funny.

"What do you do your time then?", assertively asks Robert.

"I like to watch movies and play computer games", answers Fenton with the delusion that'll fly with Robert.

"You what? Computer games? What kind of computer games and movies?", demands to know Robert. Fenton looks excited for a moment. He perks up and revels in the hope that Robert is interested in computer games too.

"Oh, I like science fiction games", quickly returns Fenton.

"Do you? You like science fiction, do you? What's that then? You watch movies about aliens wanking each other off on mars or something? Do yourself a favour lad – put the games controller down, get some fresh air, get a job and a bird. You'll feel a fucking ton better, trust me!", insists Robert.

Fenton smiles back and tells Robert he will do that. That isn't enough for Robert to leave it there though. Robert shouts out to Ryan who is now playing a game of darts in the corner of the pub, "Oi Ryan – get your mate a bird. I think he's losing the plot playing computer games about Martians. You better save him while you still can". Inevitably, Fenton blushes for a brief moment. Ryan shouts back casually while throwing darts, "Oh I am, don't worry about that. We'll get Fenton's nuts busted tonight".

Fenton overhears Ryan's plans as it's shouted to Robert from across the pub. Fenton thinks to himself if Ryan's being serious or not. Were they really going to get him hooked up with a girl tonight? Was it possible?

A couple of hours go past, and Fenton interacts with the lads on good terms. He mainly listens in on the conversations between Robert, Bill, Ryan, and Spiker more than he speaks to them. Suddenly, the lads rise up and put their jackets on. "C'mon Fenton my boy, the night is young and so are we. The fruits of the world await. Get your coat on", bursts out Ryan randomly. Before Fenton can even think or say no to anything, he finds himself wearing his jacket and following the lads into a taxi outside. It felt to Fenton like he was a small wooden stick being carried by the streams of a harsh current in a riverbed. The beer poured out and Fenton just followed the lads wherever they led him.

Sat in the cab with their seatbelts on, the lads yell amongst each other in a drunken heap. Bill pulls out his phone and starts playing nasty videos; ones of people being mutilated, like real life CCTV footage of men being torn up by a machine in a factory in some country with poor health and safety standards. All but Fenton find the videos hilarious. The cab ride comes to an end and empties out with the lads heading into a pub called, 'The Full Moon', in Harrow. "We're going to get you a bird in here Fenton", ecstatically announces Ryan. Fenton feels nervous yet optimistic and excited that Ryan may be telling the truth. What if tonight he finds a girl?

The lads head in and order pints. Fenton looks around and is overwhelmed by pretty, well-dressed girls all around him that are his age. Sticking to the bar area with the lads, Fenton stays safe. He drinks and talks to Spiker most of the time.

"Fenton, look, over there", says Spiker in a quiet tone and gestures his eyes for Fenton to look to the right. Right in the corner of the pub is an attractive blonde girl wearing a dress, peering over towards Fenton and smiling, or at least appears to be smiling in his direction. Fenton takes a look over and can't help but smile at the sight of the pretty girl. Thoughts of going over to speak to her cross his mind, until the fantasy of romance is interrupted by Ryan returning from the toilet from where he's been in there for five minutes. Doing what? Fenton didn't have a clue. He'd noticed Ryan disappear to the toilet a lot tonight. Fenton presumed that Ryan had a weak bladder.

Upon Ryan's arrival, Fenton peeks back at the pretty blonde girl in the corner, only to now behold the sight of a wicked face, displaying only disgust. The pretty girl stands up with her friends who also look outraged. Fenton is terrified for a moment, paranoid that he's stared at the girls too much and revolted them. For a moment, he thinks they are darting towards him to have a go at him. The reality, however, was they were charging to attack Ryan, who was all too familiar with those girls, on the inside and out…

The young blonde taps Ryan on the shoulder, who reacts by turning around startled and surprised. For the first time ever, Fenton sees fear expressed in Ryan's face. The group of young girls surround Ryan, where his only reaction so far is to reach out to his pint glass and down as much beer as possible. He knew that he needed it!

"You are disgusting! Leaving me standing at Victoria station for hours for you to come up with some cooked-up bollocks story, when all along you were in Sarah's pants", says the blonde girl through the top of her voice. She said it so loud that the whole pub caught her attention. It didn't help that her voice was naturally high-pitched. With her fingers having fake nails on the tips, she slaps Ryan across his face, backhand style. A couple of fake nails fly off her fingertips as the back of her hand impacts of Ryan's right side cheek.

"Right, I've heard enough of this. C'mon lads, let's go. Fenton, we're leaving", commands Ryan. Before the lads even respond, Ryan starts walking out the pub. He feels the pressure as all eyes are on him and it's a scene. The angry girls follow him out the pub yelling abuse. The young blonde girl swells up into a mixture of tears and anger at once.

"You're a little liar! Pathetic", yells out the angry blonde between the pubs doors.

"He's a fucking animal", yells out one of the other girls accompanying the enraged young lady. The lads budge past the girls and exit the pub shortly after Ryan. Robert looks immensely disappointed while Bill rolls his eyes. Spiker talks to the girls briefly to try and calm the down, with little success, where he gives up and exits the pub. Fenton runs up behind Ryan.

"What was that about? Do you know those girls?", asks Fenton while curious about what all the drama is for.

"Aye – just a silly ex. That's why I'm not with her anymore, because she's like that", answers Ryan. Fenton finds Ryan's explanation difficult to believe as it is highly likely he cheated on the young girl.

"Fuck sake Ryan, I couldn't even finish my pint", moans Robert.

"Sorry mate – I'll get you one in here to make up for it", promises Ryan to the disappointed Robert. The lads head into the next pub across the road, called Trinito.

There they find themselves in Trinito (a bar with a dark gothic feel where the walls are painted purple). Trintio was no doubt the most popular bar in Harrow. It was packed with young partygoers until early hours of the morning. Trinito's was crowded at the weekend that people were crammed between each other, and the toilets were so crowded that you couldn't take a leak without being in the middle of a conversation. Trinito's clearly didn't have the space or capacity for the crowd it drew in on the weekends. That never stopped it from being the number once place to go in Harrow for a night out. Fenton was overwhelmed by the energy of the place while intimidated by the immense crowd there. Ryan had many nights out here, while the rest of the lads stayed away. Spiker, Robert, and Bill didn't think much of Trinito. They preferred the typical pub environment with Football playing in the background.

Bill heads to the bar to order some pints. It's hard to distinguish who's next in line for a drink as the bar is surrounded by people. Bill in unsure where to even queue up. Young people flock up and down the stairs from a small entryway to the right of the bar. Upstairs is where the dancefloor is. Robert rolls his eyes at the sight of the place as it's too crowded without a seat for him to sit down on. Spiker looks excited and scans the bar for young girls, turning his head the same way a submarine periscope would turn. Meanwhile, Ryan speaks closely into Fenton's ears, trying to talk above the loud music of Trinito. He gives Fenton tips on how to behave in this place and where the toilets are.

It isn't long before a group of girls in the corner spot Ryan and pull an unpleasant facial expression. Sitting down at a table is a tall man with long, curly, ginger hair and a nose piercing. His friends look at Ryan and then lean in towards the ginger haired man. One of them points at

Ryan while yelling in the ears of this mysterious ginger haired bloke that was the centre of attention at the table he was sitting on. At that moment the ginger haired man turns his attention to Ryan with a face that turns into the very expression of anger itself. The ginger haired man's face appeared so angry, it made Fenton think of how God would look down on mankind in anger as he orders the apocalypse.

This fuming man had fiery expression that matched his perfectly fiery looking curly ginger hair. In fact, his face started to go so red with rage that he looked like he was set ablaze. It didn't help that there was a spotlight on the ceiling directly above him, highlighting the colourful display of emotion this man was going through. It truly was a face of wraith. Fenton could just picture the face in a dark storm looming over the land with red streaks of lightning as the world ended. It must have certainly had a similar effect on Ryan, who then shouted in Fenton's ear, "Oh shit. Let's get out of here!".

The same scenario played out just like it did in the previous pub, evacuation! Ryan dragged Bill away from the queue for drinks. "Fuck sake! What now?", yells Bill who is losing his patience from not being able to enjoy a pint anywhere in Harrow. Ryan is quick to gather Spiker and Robert where the lads then all exit the pub. The ginger haired bloke tries to budge past Bill by the doors of Trinito.

"Ryan. You're a dead man! Come over here now", screeches out the mysterious enraged ginger haired bloke. Before he can pass Bill, he finds Bill's large arm extend in front him, blocking him from leaving the pub, giving him no choice but to look Bill in the eyes, where Bill then tells him, "Cut it out now mate! We're not in the mood for it".

The enraged ginger yells back at Bill, "You don't understand. That bastard, that absolute little bastard, slept with my bird for months".

Bill isn't entertained or remotely interested in what that young ginger man has to say. Bill confuses the ginger bloke with, "She was never really your bird then, was she mate?". Bill then walks out Trinito's and follows the rest of the lads down the street.

Upon hearing Bill's smart remark, the furious ginger haired man relinquishes his temper for a moment and stops to think about how true Bill's words are. They do little to ease tensions though, as the ginger man soon turns temperamental again and charges out the bar after Ryan.

Robert hails a black cab from the side of the road as one comes driving past. The right indicator light of the cab flashes as it pulls up to the curb. Robert and the lads look back at Bill who is a few paces behind, find themselves startled at an enormous crowd that floods out of Trintio's behind him. The furious ginger darts towards the lads and half of Trinito's has emptied out to watch the conflict. There's a row of partygoers lined up at the end of the street holding their drinks in their hand.

"Ryan – over here you little pussyhole!", roars the ginger menace. Bill pushes him backwards where he almost trips up on the pavement. The furious ginger looks back at Bill in shock of the audacity that Bill would lay a finger on him, his eyes widened and mouth gaping open.

Bill casually looks the ginger in the eyes from behind his pair of black plastic glasses worn on his face. His eyes unflinchingly hold focus from behind the glasses lenses', confidently signalling he's serious.

"Listen you muppet – I take trains apart at six in the morning. I'll take you apart and all if you don't fuck off", threatens Bill. The enraged ginger remains quiet. Bill, convinced his threat has sunken in, casually turns around and walks towards the lads who are anxious to step inside the black cab and get away.

Whack – Bill feels knuckles smack against his head, hard. His glasses fly off his face onto the pavement. 'Ooo's' and 'aaaah's' can be heard from the crowd standing outside Trinito's as they witness the ginger whack Bill round the head.

Bill, only just coming to terms with what happened to him, picks his glasses off the floor and puts them back on his face.

"Ryan ya shitty coward. You been sleeping with Kimberly behind my back all year. Come have it out and be done with it, or I'll knock your fat mate clean out", shouts out the relentless ginger, certain of victory.

Bill is fuming and walks up to the ginger nuisance until he is in point-blank range. There, standing face-to-face with Bill, the sneaky ginger quickly throws another punch. This time, however, Bill's massive hand grips the ginger haired man's wrist before the fist can reach him. Gripping the ginger man's wrist, Bill holds it hard, then twists the ginger's arm causing him to screech.

"I warned you, you ginger shithead! Now go hit the hay ya cunt!", remarks Bill. At that very moment, Bill gets his own back by knocking the ginger menace out cold. The punch Bill throws is so hard that it makes the sound that a bowling ball makes when it hits the pins at the end of the lane for a strike. The ginger pest is no more! He drops to the ground the same way wild animal collapses after it's hit with a tranquilizer dart by hunters. Bill walks way casually like nothing happened at all, completely unmoved by the event. Crowds from Trinito's run over to the ginger who is knocked out cold on the floor. A couple of girls even scream. People start to lift out their phones to call emergency services.

The lads huddle into the cab quick.

"Driver, get us the fuck out of here", insists Spiker. The driver says nothing but starts to accelerate. Ryan is in hysterics at the sight of the knocked-out ginger. Fenton looks out the window of the moving cab in disbelief of what has transpired. He now feels nervous as the reality of how violent the lads are. He isn't sure this is the group of friends for him, but no use worrying about it now as he was locked in for the ride.

"What a muppet! If he opened his mouth one more time, I think I would have kicked his fucking appendix out!", complains Spiker while referring to the ginger nuisance.

"You see his fucking hair do? What's all that about? No wonder he lost his bird to Ryan. He looks like a bitch himself with that curly hair.", expresses Robert with his opinion on the ginger.

"Driver, take us to the West End. Step on it", drunkenly orders Spiker. Meanwhile, Bill is playing an online slot machine game on his phone, indulging in gambling having completely forgotten about the lad he knocked out cold only moments ago. That ginger could be in a coma for all Bill knew, but it was of no consolation to him though.

"Sorry Fenton – looks like someone's fucked all the birds in Harrow already. You'll just have to stick to what you're good at; wanking!", patronizingly says Robert.

Ryan looks unsettled, mixed with pride and disappointment at the same time. Now Fenton knew why Ryan stuck to that run down pub in South Harrow, he ruined his social circles in the rest of Harrow.

The black cab speeds down the road to Central London with Wembley Stadium off in the distance. The lads yelled amongst each other the whole way in their drunken frenzy.

After a tedious drive into the city, the cab driver was relieved to have the lads vacate his vehicle and leave him in peace. Robert paid him well though, giving the driver a ten-pound note as a tip.

In Leicester Square, the famous West End of London, the lads were running wild. They piled into the nearest casino and ordered cocktails. It was a lively venue they were in with the casino floors packed out. Wealthy men in suits and ties stood round roulette tables placing chips on numbers.

Stunning young women working there walked around with drinks carefully balanced on round metal trays. They wore fishnet stockings and corsets like cabaret performers. The lads couldn't take their eyes off them.

"Fuck me, look at the tits on that", comments Robert on the appearance of one of the casino workers walking by.

The lads gather around a digital display screen that streams a live video of a roulette wheel. Spiker takes the only seat in front of it, being the main contributor to the game. He pumps in twenty-pound note after twenty-pound note. The lads cheer and shout as he roulette wheels spins on the video stream followed by the white ball rolling round the edge until it finally lands on a number. Spiker's winnings and losses vary from game to game.

"Quick, Robert pick a number. Ryan, pick one!", commands Spiker.

"Eighteen", suggests Robert.

"Erm…bloody hell. Do thirty-three", blurts out Ryan.

Spiker selects multiple numbers on the screen including the ones the lads called out. The roulette wheel appears on the screen and starts spinning. The white ball lands on a number that Spiker didn't select, resulting in him winning nothing at all. Spiker then slams the screen hard with both his palms in an angry outburst at the loss of money.

"Fuuuuuuuck sake! C'mon lads – stop fucking about. Pick a bloody number that's going to win", complains Spiker.

The games go on and the lads keep calling out numbers. Fenton, however, remains quiet and observes the game. He notices a pattern reoccurring…

Every few games the same number appeared two times in a row. Fenton was making note of reoccurring numbers. Five spins ago the number seventeen was landed on twice in a row consecutively. Eight spins of the roulette wheel later, the number two was landed on by the roulette ball twice in a row. Four spins later, the number eight is landed on two spins in a row.

"C'mon you bastard! Pay out already. I must have pumped two-hundred quid into your sorry fanny by now", yells Spiker at the machine while whacking it hard again. It was as if Spiker believed the machine was a living entity that was ripping him off on purpose, and by somehow hitting it would convince the machine to let him win money. The gambling machines in this casino were designed specially to withstand physical abuse considering losing was a common occurrence.

After six spins Fenton's instincts kick in. The last number the white roulette ball landed on was number fifteen. Fenton, ecstatic with adrenaline, risked all of Spiker's money (and respect) by tapping the number fifteen on the roulette screen multiple times, until all the money Spiker had in the machine was placed on the number.

"What the bloody hell are you doing?", yells Spiker as he grabs Fenton's skinny wrist and grips it hard. Leaping out of his seat, he knocks his cocktail from the drink holder in the wooden table mounted into the roulette machine unit. The drink spills out of the cocktail glass as it hits the carpet floor of the casino, visibly dampening it.

"Have you lost the plot son? You don't gamble another man's money like that", lectures Bill to Fenton who is trapped in Spiker's tight grip.

"These social housing ones think it's alright to burn away money because they get it for fuck all on the benefits", infers Robert over Fenton's behaviour.

The Roulette wheel starts turning and the lads can't help but look at the screen. Both Fenton and Spiker look at the screen, and then look back at each other. There was fifty pounds exactly all on the number fifteen.

"If this doesn't win, you'll be leaving here with a black eye, ya pale bag of shite!", threatens Spiker to Fenton should the bet fail.

The number fifteen was the only number selected on the roulette wheel. The lads watched in anticipation as the white ball rolled round the edges of the roulette wheel that would determine Fenton's fate. Ryan watched while holding his breath in tension, just imagining Spiker walking Fenton into an alleyway in Chinatown and punching Fenton out cold into a heap of rubbish bags behind a Chinese restaurant. It even crossed Ryan's mind to start making the call for the ambulance in advance.

It seemed like the wheel was spinning forever. Round, round, round, and round it went. That fatal white ball closed in slowly. It hits the edge of a number and bounces off it, then it hits another number and bounces off that one. Finally, the roulette ball has no more momentum and lands on a number…

Fenton, unable to perceive a miracle in the making is paralyzed by the cheers and yelling of the lads. The explosion of yelling out in celebration and lads jumping up and down almost makes him drop to the floor for cover. It was like a bomb went off. The petrified Fenton is squeezed by Ryan who hugs him out of the blue. When Ryan lets go of him, Fenton has Robert and Spiker tap him on the shoulders and telling him well done. Then Fenton turned to the screen and saw the roulette ball had landed on number fifteen, just as he predicted. The winnings were well over a thousand pounds.

Spiker extends his hand out and says, "Fenton, I take it all back mate. You're a legend!".

Fenton shakes his hand.

Spiker collects the winning slip from the machine and cashes in at the desk. From that moment on, Fenton won the respect of the lads, literally (at least a fragment of respect).

The lads buy out the cocktail bar and get blind drunk.

"What did I tell you lads? I told you he was worth a chance", says Ryan who is smashed on White Russians.

"He's a fucking don! Fenton, I take it all back mate. I underestimated you. You're destined for great things", says Spiker while holding a Mojito.

"I told you Robert. You thought Fenton was a cunt! I bet you love him now", says Ryan.

"Yeah, he ain't so bad after all", unenthusiastically communicates Robert.

"Ah c'mon Robert – show him some respect. It's fucking, Fento, fucking Fenton, whatever! He's our lucky charm", spits out Spiker as the drunken mess he is.

"Alright, alright – you're a good lad", gives in Spiker while shaking Fenton's hand from across the table. Fenton smiles and gladly accepts the recognition with well-earned pina-colada in front of him.

"I'm just sorry your gay", venomously spits out Robert as he retracts from the handshake. The lads laugh at Robert's line. Fenton isn't offended too much (not while tanked on Pina Coladas). He's grateful to be at the level of respect he is at now, even if it hasn't stopped the insults towards him.

With the miracle winnings that Fenton made possible, the lads head out on a pub crawl in soho going between cocktail bars.

They finish the night by heading back to South Harrow in a black cab.

The lads head back to Robert's house where they congregate in his kitchen drinking beers and talking nonsense into the night. Fenton is astonished by Robert's house and how comfortable it looks. It looks like a luxury bar. The living room has a faux leather sofa lined up in front of a giant H.D T.V screen pinned to the wall on brackets across the room. The kitchen work top was made of white granite with white wooden metal-based bar stools around it. Exploring further, Fenton walks up to Robert's back door, looking out the integrated double-glazed windowpane to Robert's garden. Fenton was impressed at the sight of the back garden, especially the outdoor swimming pool that was fitted in. While Fenton is looking outside, Robert notices him inspecting the garden through the window of the back door, and interrupts Fenton with, "Impressed with my garden are ya?".

"Oh yes Robert. This place is fantastic. I love what you've done to the place", compliments Fenton.

While holding a beer bottle and looking all doll-eyed and drunk, Robert says to Fenton, "You ever pull your soft bollocks together and get a job, you might be able to buy a place like this one day...maybe!".

Spiker pulls out a folded-up piece of paper, then unwraps it on the surface of Robert's kitchen worktop. White powder scattered all over it where Spiker then uses his bank card to separate the white powder into lines. What was it though? Fenton asked himself in the privacy of his thoughts. It looked like washing up powder. Then it occurred to Fenton that it was cocaine. This made him nervous, wanting to leave immediately. It was half past two in the morning though. It would take Fenton forever to get back to Camden Town from South Harrow this early in the morning with the Underground trains not running.

Spiker pulled out a ten-pound-note from his pocket and rolled it into a straw-like shape. The next step was using the rolled-up note to sniff the white powder, which was most certainly cocaine.

Spiker hands the tenner to Ryan who sniffs a line. In the aftermath of sniffing, Ryan turns around slowly with widened eyes and dilated pupils. He smiles dementedly while off his nut on cocaine before acting all strange and laughing hysterically out the blue. Next to sniff the cocaine is Bill who doesn't seemed affected at all. Same goes for Robert who sniffs a line like it's a cup of coffee through the same ten-pound-note. The moment Fenton's been dreading comes into play, where Ryan takes the tenner and holds out towards Fenton, gesturing him to sniff a line.

"No thanks man, that's not my thing", declines Fenton.

"Don't be rude! Spiker's offering you a line. It's bad manners to turn down a line", insists Ryan. Fenton turns shaky and anxious as the peer pressure is overwhelming. He doesn't want to say yes, but he's too scared to say no. Fenton stands there rotating looks at the lads hoping they will cut him some slack.

"Fenton! Do the bloody the line, now!", firmly demands Ryan in a monstrous frown. The aura around Ryan was intense and Fenton had never seen him appear so menacing and aggressive.

The peer pressure was too much for Fenton, who gave in and took the ten-pound note to sniff the line.

"Good man", says Spiker in support of Fenton having a sniff.

Fenton stands over the line that is perfectly straightened and ready to be sniffed. He breathes in deep from nerves. Holding the tenner at the end of the line, he leans in and places the end of his nose to the other end of the ten-pound-note, then sniffs hard, vacuuming the cocaine off the kitchen worktop like a living hoover. When Fenton pulls his head up, he looks down to see the kitchen worktop devoid of any white powder. His nose feels numb. Suddenly, he's rushed with a euphoric feeling. He feels elevated and overwhelmed. The lads cheer. There's a strange feeling in his throat. It's like he has a panic attack. Fenton runs out the kitchen and straight upstairs to Robert's toilet. He kneels onto the bathroom floor and vomits in the toilet bowl. While he throws up, Fenton can hear Ryan giggling outside the bathroom door.

"Hahaha you ain't? Please tell me you ain't in there throwing up after one line?", asks Ryan while Fenton is busy throwing up. Fenton is too sick to answer Ryan and wishes he'd just leave him alone. The stimulation from the cocaine was too much. However, Fenton felt a world better after being sick.

Fenton walks out the bathroom and meets a coked-up Ryan who gives him a hug. The two head back downstairs to the lads in the kitchen.

"It's alright lads, Fenton just had to let out some of his guts. He's doing much better now", reassures Ryan.

"He better not have thrown up on my bathroom floor or he can go up there and mop it", miserably says Robert with his arms folded, leaning against his fridge/freezer.

Fenton feels like he can take on the world after the first line, before he knows it, he's sniffing another one, followed by another line shorty after that. The lads pass the same ten-pound note between each other all night.

Ryan sniffs a line which results in him roaring like Tarzan and pounding his own chest like an ape. Fenton gets louder and more talkative the more lines he takes. The lads while coked-up talk about all sorts of rubbish, things they wouldn't even be interested in talking about when sober. Fenton is having the best night of his life. He's talking, talking, and laughing away with the lads. It was almost perfect, almost…

Ryan's phone rings. It's his girlfriend. After a brief phone call, Ryan pops out and brings his girlfriend to Robert's kitchen. She was a gorgeous redhead who was also a cocaine sniffer. Ryan introduces her to Fenton and the lads.

Fenton quietens down and his mood lowers. Standing there drunk and high on cocaine, time seems to drag for eternity as he must witness Ryan's relationship first-hand. This redheaded girl sniffs line after line and kisses Ryan in the corner of the kitchen. The conversation only flows between Fenton and the rest of the lads, while Ryan has cut himself off while jumping into a romantic bubble.

The redhead goes upstairs to the bathroom. Ryan pulls out a condom from his wallet and waves it around in front the lads with a crazed face like he's lost the plot.

"Time to end the night with a busted set of nuts", hints Ryan with dilated pupils from all the cocaine, still waving the condom left and right like he's flying a kite with it.

"Good lad, smash her. Get your mate a bird too. He looks like he needs one", says Spiker in reference to Fenton.

"Oh aye mate – don't worry Fenton, we'll get ya a bird, even if she's on the large side of life, if you know what I mean?", mockingly promises Ryan. Then he bursts out laughing like a maniac or bad guy from a James Bond movie. Suddenly, the redheaded beauty returns from upstairs, where Ryan's face suddenly switches shape into a serious and in control boyfriend. Ryan puts his arm round her and heads off to do his own business. He says farewell to the lads before leaving.

Now Fenton was left alone with Robert, Spiker, and Bill. He sniffs some more lines with them. Standing there high as a kite, Fenton looks over at Robert who is also high as a kite.

"Living on fucking benefits wanking all night and day. Pick up a fucking shovel or something and make yourself useful", thoroughly advises Robert regarding Fenton's lack of employment. This was the last thing on Fenton's mind however, as the lack of a girlfriend was a much bigger concern to him.

"Get a bird Fenton. You're a top lad. Just be nice to a bird, talk to her a bit, then you can walk off with your arm round her, instead of that silly bollocks", advises Spiker.

The sun comes up and brightens up Robert's kitchen. Fenton leaves the house and walks all the way up Harrow Hill and down the other side to Harrow-On-The-Hill tube station. Sitting on the Metropolitan Line at the crack of dawn, paranoid from being so coked up, Fenton stares out the window feeling low. The feeling was probably just the come down from the drugs and alcohol. Fenton knew in his heart he felt miserable and lonely, wishing he could put his arm round a girl and head back to hers for a night the same way Ryan did with that redhead. In that coked up moment at three-thirty in the morning, Ryan promised Fenton a bird. Was it possible? Fenton didn't think so, but things were getting increasingly interesting hanging out with Ryan.

Fenton would see what else Ryan could produce…

Chapter 5: Incendia

At home, Fenton is putting on his brand-new clothes that Ryan bought him last weekend. Looking fresh and feeling confident, Fenton is ready to have another adventurous night with his new friends. In his pocket is a wallet loaded with four hundred pounds. Spiker let him have that money from the big win Fenton pulled off in the casino last weekend. Smiling at his own reflection, Fenton is impressed with himself. Never in the history of his life has he had that much money in his wallet. Only a week ago he was a broke, scruffy, loner. Thanks to Ryan, he managed to turn it around.

Fenton heads downstairs and puts on his coat that is hanging over the stair railing. While putting it on, his father (drunk on whiskey as usual) notices Fenton about to head outside. Sitting there in the same filthy stained white vest day by day, his father smokes from morning until night, letting out fumes like a factory chimney. A rocks glass half full of scotch whisky accompanied by a glass ash tray is resting on top of the aged, dark shaded wooden table next to the armchair his father is sitting in. The armchair looks no better either with its worn looking condition apparent by loose threads from the ageing upholstery.

"Don't you be out too late", says his father, just able to speak before erupting into coughing. Clearly, the alcohol and smoking were rotting his father's voice box day by day. It was a surprise his father didn't launch into a frenzy of verbal abuse like he normally does. Supposedly, his father was proud to see Fenton looking smart and going out to see friends, even though he never expressed these thoughts to Fenton.

"I won't Dad. You can call me if you're worried about me", reassures Fenton. Within an instant Fenton slips out the front door and is already excited by the fresh night air. Looking up at the sky above, the stars are visible along with half the moon lit up. There was a good vibe channelled in Fenton where he could feel that only good things awaited tonight.

Sitting on the London Underground tube carriage, Fenton watched buildings lit up in the dark as the train rode past them. Wembley Stadium, with its arc lit up overhead, gleamed over the surrounding area. The train journey continued onwards until Fenton could see the church spire of Harrow Hill lit up with bright orange lights surrounding it. The orb-like red light shone unmistakably at the very top of the spire. Harrow Hill appeared as if it were growing from Fenton's view as the train neared. Finally, the London Underground train reached Harrow-on-the-Hill station, where Fenton made his way out and started walking to South Harrow.

After a familiar walk over the top of Harrow Hill and through South Harrow, Fenton finds himself pushing open the door to O'Conner's pub. The lads and Ryan are seated around the table drinking pints. There's two men serving from behind the bar, other groups of overweight middle-aged men drinking pints as expected. Almost everything in O'Conner's looks normal, almost...

Something distracts Fenton from the corner of the pub, an image that is blooming, standing out like a bright star of the sky he gazed at on the walk here.

Fenton is stunned! He is left awestruck and dazzled by this unexpected sight of fine visual appearance. What he saw was so colourful and bright, not fitting in to any of the surroundings of the pub. It was like a flowering rose bud at the end of a long stem that somehow grew out of thorny hedges. There was no other way to describe it. The breath-taking sight was a woman. Not just any woman, possibly the most beautiful one that Fenton had ever seen.

This woman was practically everything Fenton ever wanted in a woman, at least in appearance. She was a slender gothic doll with long black hair, that was messy, just the way Fenton liked it. It was a scruffy look that Fenton found attractive. Her pale skin was smooth and beaming with an inviting radiance. Piercings covered her face and ears with all sorts of metal studs attached. Black fishnet tights covered her legs, leading down to the most unique pair of high heel shoes Fenton had have ever seen. They were almost made entirely of steel. This woman's metal heels were exquisitely crafted into gothic patterns and spikes. The shoes looked like weapons someone would wear on their feet. The clothing she wore was a tattered black skirt (nothing special) and a red jumper that matched her red lipstick. The unique dress style of this woman was contradicting to itself. The mysterious goth lady looked gorgeous, trashy, scary, sexy, and dangerous all at once.

Fenton could only stop and watch in astonishment as he tried to figure out this beautiful woman that was so puzzling and alluring. He watched her drink red wine with her legs crossed, sitting in-between two middle aged men with grey hair that looked miles out of her league.

The mysterious beauty sitting down in the corner of the pub stuck out with her red jumper that tightly fitted her, compared to the black and grey jackets, and brown and grey jumpers every man wore in the pub. Her petite figure was as artfully crafted as any beautiful doll of a woman could be, leaving Fenton wanting to hold her immediately. To him, she was as an adorable deer that's fur would comfort you the moment you stroked it. It was painful for him to watch as the desire and lust for this mysterious goth was overwhelming. The blissful daydream of immediate romance was a bubble quickly popped by Ryan, who called out, "Fenton, over here you dopey cunt!".

The lads laughed as Fenton stood gormlessly in the middle of the pub gazing at the corner, like a cow standing in the middle of a field, unsure what to do with itself. He snapped out of the seductive spell and went to join the lads. They are happy to see him. Spiker heads up to the bar and orders pints for all of them. A couple of pints in, Fenton is stuck in conversations going backwards and forwards about the usual topics such as football and violence. Bill recounts a tale from where a young group of men tried to mug him earlier in the week, to which resulted in the assaulters being knocked out. You knew the story was true because Bill's knuckles were bruised badly.

Fenton struggles to keep up with the conversation of the lads that becomes all too boring when compared to the beauty and wonder of a woman. The mysterious goth captures his attention again, as she treads in those platform high heels made of steel. They are like anchors on her feet. The goth girl, however, somehow can tread so lightly in them. Fenton wonders how her thin legs that look as delicate as deer's, has the power to pull those blocks of metal-like heels up down from the floor. There she is, leaning over the bar with her long black hair hanging over her face, bottom pressed out like a bubble about to pop. Her tender legs wrapped in fishnet tights are towering. The barman pours her a glass of red wine, where she pays for it before treading gently on the pub carpet in those monstrous shoes back to where she was sitting.

Ryan clicks his fingers in front of Fenton's face, before yelling, "Oi, you dopey shite, wake up! What's wrong with ya?". Fenton almost jumps as his sublime moment of admiring the sheer beauty of the gothic woman is abruptly interrupted. Bill laughs. Robert shakes his head in his usual way of shaking his head at Fenton, indicating he looks down on him as always. "You been smoking that reefer or something mate?", asks Robert.

"I'm only tired is all. Nothing to bother about", is the excuse Fenton makes up. He drinks more beer from his pint glass and makes an effort to catch up on what the lads are saying. While the evening continues and Fenton consumes more pints with the lads, his attention only becomes more fixated on this hellish beauty.

The gothic lady catches Fenton's eye when he notices her getting up again and heading down to the corridor to the lady's toilets. He tries to ignore the sight of her, until he spots her walking out from the corridor, elegantly placing one leg in front of the other as she does. She walked so well composed like a model on a catwalk. In-between that messy black hair was the pierced face of an angel of darkness, all her studs and piercings reflecting the lights off the pub ceiling. Fenton was hypnotized by this twisted goddess that looked like an angel kicked out of heaven for getting too drunk all the time. For the moment that Fenton's eyes met her walking head on from where he was facing, it seemed to him like everything surrounding her dimmed down. All brightness and colour around her seemed to fade, while she stood brightly above everything around her. Fenton's mind was playing tricks on him where she seemed to be moving in almost slow motion. In that moment she was the centre of Fenton's world, where all sound was blocked out from his attention. It was like he went completely deaf. Only this cruel figure of beauty that teased all of Fenton's senses existed to him now. She was like a sun that shone bright in deep space with nothing else surrounding but pure darkness. She was the source of everything that had any depth of feeling to it at all. Nothing else around him right now was even worth its own existence.

Ryan slaps Fenton hard across the face, so hard you could hear the smack like a firecracker going off. "Wake up for fuck sake! Daydreaming away over there – stay at home if you're going to do that", complains Ryan. The lads laugh.

The evening continues, and Fenton focuses his mental discipline away from the lustful thoughts of the mysterious woman. He thinks to himself that there's no need to concern himself with such temptation. The dark angel in the pub that's dressed like a prostitute would surely have no interest in Fenton anyhow. There was no need to torture himself with delusions and fantasies of romance.

Spiker, Bill, and Robert left the pub temporarily to get supplies for Robert's kitchen. They'd need beers and other things (drugs) for later. Leaving just Ryan and Fenton in O'Conner's, the two engaged in conversation about their favourite computer game, Timetrippers 2. They laughed as they recalled the characters that were playable in the video game.

"Let's get a shot Fenton. Come on, let's see what's at the bar", demands Ryan. The two walk up to the bar where they analyse what spirits are available on the glass shelved display of bottles. Fenton, deep in concentration over what may be the most suitable shot for him and Ryan to drink, has his ears invaded by a loud voice of a woman. It was her…

"Good evening Mr Ryan, how do you do?", says the pretty gothic lady.

"Oh, hey love. I'm grand, how ya been? It's been a while now", answers Ryan.

Fenton is overwhelmed with mixed feelings. He's excited he's this close to the woman, yet frustrated Ryan may already have his fingers in the pie. Ryan and the goth chat for a few moments. Out of nowhere Ryan turns around and says, "This is my mate, Fenton. Just giving him a good old tour of the pubs of South Harrow".

It was then that goth beauty tilted her head slightly to the right to see past Ryan's shoulder to get a sight of Fenton's visage.

"Why, hello there Mr...I haven't seen you around here before", says the goth in a cockney-style accent.

"Hello", Fenton squeaks back. Looking directly at the pretty woman's visage decorated in metal piercings, Fenton is swallowed by the beauty of her. His heart beats like a steam engine. His cheeks have turned bright red as he's completely flustered. Looking into her eyes, brown like polished wood, somehow appearing laminate and shiny, Fenton's heart and soul explodes. It's as if he was shot in the chest by an arrow then and there.

"Where are you from then? What brings you this way?", demands to know the gothic angel. Fenton answers typically. He tells her he's just here for drinks with his friend. The gothic beauty laughs, laughs, and laughs her arse off at the encounter she has with Fenton. This makes him almost pass out from a panic attack.

"There's something about you, boy!", remarks the wicked goth through her lipstick covered mouth and slippery moist tongue with a piercing right on the tip of it.

Ryan buys the three of them a shot of sambuca, then craftly walks off to use the toilets, leaving Fenton alone. The shot gives Fenton some liquid courage to continue talking to the gothic princess that he so desires more than anything else in the world.

Fenton and the goth get to know each other as any two would. They get the usual chat out the way by asking what they each do for a living, so on and so forth. The boring talk is put aside by the electric flirting moves that the goth advances on Fenton with.

"You got nice hair ya know", says the gothic flirt as she strokes the hair on Fenton's head with her fingers painted black, each with a gothic steel ring on. While Fenton is groomed instantly, his eyes almost roll back in euphoria from this seductress's fine touch, succumbing him to her devilry without any resistance. He can only pause and take a deep breath as his dreams appear to be coming true. The goth giggles at Fenton, who is nothing more than a rabbit stuck in the headlights.

The pair sat on a stall each in front of the bar. Fenton embraces the wholesome flesh of this woman that is placed on top of the bar stool the same way a piece of meat cooks on top of a lit barbecue. She was lit up like she was on fire in terms of her glamour. Fenton couldn't help but look her up and down every moment, admiring the skin and flesh of her crossed legs under those fishnet tights. All of her movements were alluring and flirtatious. There was an art form to this woman's body language.

Fenton was smiling and laughing away as the goth mainly lead the conversation on, talking non-stop about a hundred different topics. Fenton didn't really care about what she had to say, he was riding on a high, leeching off her powerful energy and confidence.

Ryan sat down at the table they were at before with the lads returned. Briefly, he peeks back at the table to see the lads laughing at him as he's stuck in the goth's grasp. He can't figure out why they are so amused. It's of little consequence to him either way, he's too busy being seduced to think about anything or anyone else around him. It's tunnel vision all the way!

It's late now. Fenton's been talking to this goth angel all night. Only a handful of people are left in the pub, the biggest group being Ryan and the lads. O'Conner's pub has that quietness to it that all pubs have when they are about to close for the night. The music has stopped playing. The pub lights are turned up brighter, and the clashes of pint glasses being stacked into the dishwasher under the bar are heard. It was time to go home.

"I hate to ask, but I get followed sometimes when it's late. Would you walk me home?", sweetly asks the goth. Fenton doesn't really have a choice, not in his mind anyway. What the beautiful goth asks for, the beautiful goth gets. Fenton was already enslaved.

After the goth seductress puts on her black denim jacket, Fenton escorts her out the pub, oblivious to Ryan and the rest of the lads. Before he can make it out the door, Spiker yells out, "Go on Fenton my son! Don't forget to use a condom". Fenton, whose attention is entirely fixated on his newfound goddess, ignores Spiker's yelling with ease.

Walking down the street from O'Conner's pub, Fenton feels like he's floating on a cloud. The goth's metal high heels can be heard thudding against the pavement with every step she takes. It looked like they'd crack the pavement any moment.

"Those shoes are really something. Aren't they difficult to walk in?", curiously asks Fenton.

"No more difficult than life itself", answers the gothic goddess.

Fenton walks her so far before she stops and tells him he doesn't need to walk any further. The two of them pause while facing each other, standing below a lit-up streetlight that illuminated the area. All was still and silent around them. Only parked cars outside terraced houses occupied the road.

Fenton looked into the lush brown eyes of the gothic beauty, his heart pounding away. She was so close to his face that he could smell her red wine scented breath. Before Fenton even has a second to contemplate what's happening, the woman has leaned and smashed her lips against his and extended her tongue down his throat. He grabs the back of her head and grips her hair, and kisses away as he does. The kissing goes on and on, where Fenton can't get enough of her. He strokes her face, feeling the studs across her nose and cheeks like a blind man reading brail. The touch of her soft skin stuns him. Wasting no time, he strokes all of her. Fenton strokes her back, then he gently places his hand on her hips, admiring her thin waste. The moment he's been itching for the most, he strokes her legs, those smooth legs wrapped under the fishnet tights. The remarkable legs that look soft as jelly, yet somehow are firm enough to lift those steel heels up down off the ground, heels that prop her up like she's on a pedestal. Fenton's almost fully aroused. He wants to rip those fishnet tights off her.

The goth retracts her tongue from his mouth, then the two hug each other. Fenton feels fully consoled with the warmth of this goddess in his arms. Her softness comforts him the same way a soft toy would to a four-year-old boy. He squeezes her, not wanting to let go of this precious doll, ever.

"I don't know what it is about you Fenton, but you're really special", says the goth while holding onto Fenton. Eventually, the two let go, then look at each other smiling, both unable to contain their happiness, especially Fenton.

The two arrange to meet again next week. The gothic model walks off in those demon-like high heels that could smash a window in if she kicked one with them. Fenton watches her walk off, staring at the back of her in obsession like a crazed pervert.

"Wait...", Fenton calls out. The petite goth turns around. "What is your name? I still don't know", asks Fenton.

"Incendia", answers the goth in a powerful tone, like a queen of the underworld announcing her title to a thousand doomed souls. Then she walks off delicately, balancing herself on those demonic high heels.

Fenton heads back to O'Conner's pub completely dazed and sure that he's fallen in love. He smiles all the way back to the pub feeling over the moon he's just had his first kiss. He's met the girl of his dreams. Incendia was the twisted goth doll that he thought only existed in his wet dreams. Incendia...Incendia...repeats Fenton in his mind. He's obsessed with the name already. It's the first time he's met a girl called Incendia. The unique name matches how unique the gothic woman is, thinks Fenton. All he can do is think about her on the walk back to the pub, his mind completely absorbed by thoughts of her. He's so hijacked by Incendia that he almost gets himself run over twice on the walk back to the pub, unable to focus on anything else other than her. Everything around Fenton was all so wonderful, where the pavement seemed all the smoother, and the streetlights all the brighter, with the sky appearing all the clearer. It must be love...

Fenton strolls back into O'Conner's with a grin on his face. The lads give him a round of applause, then he sits down beside them. Ryan, sitting beside him, rustles Fenton's hair and squeezes him with a one-armed hug round the shoulders.

"That's my boy. You've scored", declares Ryan in celebration to Fenton.

"Why didn't you go back home with her and get it on?", asks Bill. Fenton shrugs and says, "I don't know her well enough yet".

"You don't wanna know her here either, she's a fucking nutter. Just get your leg over and be done with it", advises Spiker, sitting across the table.

"What the fuck do you want date her for anyway? She's a weirdo. You must be weird too to want to date her", rants Robert.

"Oi, leave him alone. He's scored. A hole is a goal. Let it be…", comments Ryan.

The lads finish their pints and put their coats on. They all head back to Robert's house and sniff cocaine off his kitchen worktop all night until the sun rises.

Fenton sniffs cocaine and pounds his chest like a gorilla. He's laughing all night long while chatting garbage with Ryan. The lads are so coked up that the slightest thing is hilarious to them. Fenton, he's on top of the world, high on gear and rejoicing in what he expects to be a newfound relationship with Incendia. Ryan hands him a condom and wishes him good luck for his next date.

Robert, coked up from sniffing lines all night, leans against his kitchen worktop, pupils dilated and looking numb. He calls out to Fenton with, "Right, you daft cunt! I want to have a word with you". The whole kitchen goes silent and the lads stop laughing for once.

"Now you think you're on top and about to get ya bollocks drained, but normally when somethings too good to be true, it isn't fucking true", speaks out Robert, looking spot on at Fenton.

Smirking while out of his head on gear, Fenton doesn't take Robert seriously. He has come to expect nothing but insults from Robert either way. Fenton has come to expect criticism over his new relationship from the lads.

"You didn't think a clown like you would have a serious relationship with a girl like that, did ya? She's lost her marbles. The bird comes in tarted up every weekend milking victim after victim, like yourself, for money and attention. Don't be a puppet, you stupid cunt. Wake up!", firmly speaks out Robert. Bill nods in agreement to Robert's little speech.

"Honestly, Fenton, she's a piss taker. Me and Robert see her every weekend in O'Conner's with a different bloke. Get ya leg over and then fuck her out of your life for good", advises Spiker.

"That's not all Spiker. Someone tell him what happened to them lads…", strangely brings up Bill out of the blue.

"I didn't want to tell you this mate, it might scare ya. There's been a few blokes that dated her that lost the plot, isn't that right Spiker?", says Robert.

"Too right Robert. Remember Shane McDonough? He had a big stand off when he came into the pub to find her dating another bloke. The poor lad lost it, smashed the pub windows in a temper over her", explains Spiker, recounting the tale.

"That poor bloke got arrested and charged, all while that tart that broke his heart walked away without a fucking scratch", adds Bill to the tale, recounting it from memory.

"That ain't the only one. Remember Jimmy Doyle? He was a single mug like Fenton. The cunt got obsessed with her and emptied out five credit cards just to take her out on dates. He started to go mad when she stopped showing up at the pub. Rumour has it, the twat knew what street she lived in, but not what house. The idiot went knocking on door to door asking for her every night. The shithead grew so desperate to see her again, he started breaking into houses to try and find her. One night the old bill arrested him, no one's seen him since. A few lads say he's been sectioned in the nut house. Rumour has it, he's screaming her name out loud all night in a padded cell", tells Robert with a stern face, expressing the utmost seriousness of the matter.

Fenton, still feeling high from the coke, turns to look at Spiker and Bill, who also look dead serious over the matter. They stand there, also coked out of their head with dilated pupils, with their arms crossed in seriousness of what they are telling Fenton.

Ryan can't help but burst out laughing. "Nah – you lot are out of order. Let Fenton be for fuck sake. Let him have his fun", giggles Ryan.

"Oi – silly bugger – if you want to protect that numb bollocks of a mate of yours, I suggest you listen to what we're saying", says Robert loudly to Ryan.

Spiker walks up to Fenton and puts his arm round him, and then says, "Fenton, mate, you're a top bloke. You got a lot going for ya. You'll find better birds than her. Soak her panties out and close a lid on it after that, you got that mate?".

Spiker grips his arm around Fenton hard, looking right into his face waiting for a reply, appearing as if he won't release his grip until he gets the right answer.

"Yeah Spiker, sure. I won't go deep with her. It'll just be a one-night stand thing", says Fenton in a shaky voice.

Spiker taps him on the shoulder, says, "Good man – you're my boy, you know that? You ever have any trouble; I'll be here for ya mate". Fenton smiles and thanks Spiker.

Fenton walks over Harrow Hill, feeling anxious and intoxicated from heavy drug use. He is still smiling to himself. The unmistakable feeling of true love is flowing through him like blood flowing in his veins. Thinking about what the lads told him about Incendia, he laughs out loud in the quiet street. What a heap of lies, Fenton thinks to himself. Surely, the lads are jealous he's scored a beautiful goth girl that they probably fantasize about in their dreams. Fenton concludes that the lads are just trying to scare him with tales and lies out of jealously and spite.

Those lads just want to see him miserable and unhappy. They just want to ruin it for him because they can't have her for themselves, Fenton thinks on the walk back to Harrow tube station. He laughs about the tales of a bloke getting sectioned because he was so obsessed over Incendia. Bullshit! Fenton smiles, expecting to have a long-lasting relationship with her…

Chapter 6: Deep Black

Standing at the bar in O'Conner's, Fenton orders a wine for Incendia and a pint for himself. While the drinks are poured out, he looks back at Incendia who is sitting by the window near the pub entrance, with her legs stretched out on the pub seating. Tonight, she's dressed like a prostitute out of hell just like she was dressed last time. This time she's dressed in a more generic purple gothic look, rather than the blend of passionate red and black mixture style clothing she wore last weekend. Fenton, completely enamoured by Incendia's smooth legs wrapped in black fishnet tights, gawks at her while she's laid out like a cat stretching out on its owner's sofa. Smiling while completely captivated by Incendia's attractive body, Fenton's divine moment is interrupted by cruel laughing he hears from the end of the bar.

The lads are all gathered in a group at the end of the bar. It's Ryan, Bill, Robert and Spiker, all laughing at Fenton as they observe him buy drink after drink for Incendia. They're hunched together judging Fenton while holding their pints. It was as if the were allocated as a jury for the pub, passing down judgement on Fenton for every wine he purchased for Incendia.

"What the fuck does he think he's doing?", says one of the lads. Fenton can't figure out who said it, although it was most likely Robert. It takes all his discipline to ignore the lads and focus his attention on Incendia. Fenton knew that interacting with the lads would only bring his confidence down. He didn't need that. Carrying a glass of wine and a pint, Fenton turns his back on the lads and brings the drinks to Incendia. Tonight, she's wearing something unique – it's a metal pentagram accessory she wears on a thin metal chain round her neck. The pentagram accessory looks heavy as it dangles from her delicate neck.

Fenton sits down and Incendia leans back on him, where he then puts his arms round her waist. Never in his life has there been such a blissful feeling for him. He strokes Incendia's messy black hair like she's his pet.

"You're great to lean on", says Incendia as she gently strokes Fenton's thigh with her black painted nails.

"You…you feel great", compliments Fenton in return.

Incendia giggles before saying, "Your voice is so posh. I love it. Is that even your real voice? I think you're just putting it on".

"Honest, this is my voice", says Fenton.

"I fucking love it", dominantly declares Incendia as she squeezes Fenton's thigh tighter with her hands. Fenton can't let go of her. He's addicted to holding her body and stroking her hair.

"You're so hot", says Fenton in feeble way that is the equivalent of waving a white flag in the air. He'd succumbed to her beauty and wasn't afraid to admit it. The inner animal within him was loose. For hours they'd talk about movies, television series, and music. They talked about their favourite bands. Incendia, being older than Fenton by a few years, talked about seeing bands he didn't have the chance to see these days. Incendia had seen all the best metal bands live.

Fenton loses himself in the night with Incendia. Nothing else or anyone else around him was important. Stuck there gripping her tight, he couldn't keep his eyes off her legs that lay stretched out in front of him. He couldn't resist the comfort of her divine touch as she was flopped over him. Fenton stroked her hair with his fingers, over, over, and over again. Then he hugged her waist hard and listened to her talk into the night. The pair of them talked about everything.

Fenton got up to get more drinks for the pair of them. "Cunt must be spending every last dime he's got on that cow", says a voice from the end of the bar. Fenton ignores it. He carries drinks back to Incendia.

Now the alcohol hits Fenton's head, Incendia's too. Before he knows it, the talking comes to a halt, and the physical interaction fires up...

Incendia holds Fenton's hand and moves it over her legs. His rolls back as he almost gets erect from the soft touch of them. More laughing can be heard from the bar where the lads are, but Fenton doesn't care. He knows he's being laughed at. The moment is too good to let what people think of it get in the way.

Incendia moves her head back and Fenton leans in forwards. The two of them kiss wildly, where Fenton then strokes her face, feeling the piercings on it. The stud at the end of her tongue rolls on the tip of his tongue while they make out. Then Fenton strokes her legs, gripping those fishnet tights with the urge to rip them off. He's totally engrossed in her and strokes her until his hands meet back of her neck, where he then grips it hard.

Incendia pulls her head back and speaks gently into Fenton's ear, saying, "This is a shithole. Everyone in here is boring, apart from you. I'm sick of that pack of overweight dumb arses laughing at you from over there".

Fenton turns his head slightly to see the lads talking to each other while looking in his direction, all making fun of him, mean grins across their face.

"Don't look at them", says Incendia to Fenton, knowing he's turned his head by feeling his jaw brush against her cheeks.

"They're not very good mates", says Incendia in disappointment.

"Them? I...I...only met them week before last...", hesitantly explains Fenton.

"Then they're piss all, ain't they?", abruptly blurts out Incendia. Fenton doesn't know what to say. Incendia leans back so she can look Fenton in the eyes. He gazes back at her twisted beauty, a face so innocently beautiful, yet pale and haunting with piercings. His heart flutters as those shining brown eyes splinter his soul, looking directly into his own blue eyes. Then she places her soft hand on his cheek, full of thick metal rings on each finger, appearing like she's wearing a knuckle duster. The soft bony fingers of hers stroke Fenton's face along with the coldness that comes with the metal rings on them. While she holds his face, she looks into his eyes and says, "They're jealous of you. They know I will take you to the realm of pleasure", mysteriously says Incendia.

"The realm of pleasure?", mumbles Fenton in confusion, gawking at Incendia, blatantly seduced by the moment.

"Yes – the realm of pleasure", seductively whispers Incendia.

"What? What do you mean by that? What is the realm of pleasure?", asks Fenton, desperate to know.

"You'll find out tomorrow my love", answers Incendia while maintaining a seductive tone to her voice. Those dark red lipstick smothered lips of hers shape into a deviant smile. Fenton could only blush. This could only mean one thing...he was going to lose his virginity.

Incendia retracts her hand from Fenton's blushing cheek, leaving him completely flustered. Her smile disappears as her face shifts back to a sterner and more serious look.

"We're going down Camden Town tomorrow. There's loads of bars we can go to for a drink. It'll be fun. You know it will better than sitting here with them taking the piss outta you. They ain't ya mates Fenton. Promise me you won't listen to a word them melons say about me. They'll try and keep you apart from me because they're miserable. Do you understand what I'm saying?", boldly tells Incendia to Fenton while still looking directly into his eyes.

"I understand. They won't get in the way", reassuringly answers Fenton without any hesitation at all. He smiles while still holding eye contact. Incendia smiles back again, says, "Good, lovely! I got a really good feeling about us being together. This is going to be really special to me. You're special Fenton, you ain't like other blokes. You ain't like those low lives in the corner over there just downing pint after pint and talking football all day. You're unique", Incendia tells Fenton.

The two put their arms round each other, and Fenton squeezes her hard and lovingly.

"You're the most beautiful and astonishing woman I've met Incendia. I want to be with you more than anything", groans out Fenton who is still succumbed to her charms and flirtatious actions. The two kiss each other intensely while holding each other tight. Incendia adjusts herself so she's sitting on Fenton's crotch. Immediately, Fenton is overwhelmed. He desperately tries to resist becoming aroused but finds it impossible. Incendia grabs his wrist and moves his hand up her skirt until it strokes her bottom. Having permission to do so, Fenton places both his hands up her skirt and squeezes her bottom through the fishnet leggings of hers. He can do nothing else but kiss her, unable to resist her by the slightest. Fenton lets himself go completely and strokes her bottom and legs until he reaches her feet. He can't help but stroke those steel heels of hers, curious to how heavy and solid they are. Incendia towers over him, her bottom stuck to his lap, her head leaning down to kiss him while her hands slide through his hair as passionately. Fenton isn't afraid to be seen getting intimate with Incendia. She was too good to turn down, no matter how much the lads laughed about it as they watched from across the pub.

Later that evening, Fenton walked Incendia home. Holding her hand all the way back to the street she lived in, the pair of them stop. They kiss each other while hugging. Spontaneously, Incendia drops to the pavement and pulls Fenton's arm as she tells him to drop down with him. He dared not disobey his dark goddess, so he lay down on the pavement beside her.

Incendia and Fenton lay out in the middle of the pavement looking up at the stars.

"Just keep watching", lightly speaks out Incendia who lays out straight next to Fenton. This made him uncomfortable laying here in the street. Not only was the concrete uncomfortable, but he couldn't relax knowing someone walking their dog could step on them as they pass. However, all seems quiet. Fenton starts to relax now. Holding Incendia's hand, he gazes up at the stars. The purple night sky matches Incendia's clothing today. Fenton gets lost in the sight of the stars as they twinkle and shine brightly. The warmth and love of Incendia combined with the awe-striking night sky of stars consoles him. He just lay there smiling while leaning back on the pavement with Incendia, feeling happy, entirely.

Time passed and Incendia went home, still not letting Fenton see what house she lived in. That was fair enough thought Fenton. He was still a stranger to her and maybe she didn't want to reveal such things to him.

Fenton made his way back into O'Conner's pub and joined the lads, still at the end of the bar. They laughed at him the moment he entered.

Ryan gives him a hug and says, "That's my boy. Have you done the deed yet?".

"The what?", asks Fenton in his ignorance.

"You know, the deed. Have you boned her yet?", boldly asks Ryan.

"No…man", hesitantly answers back Fenton, unsure how to answer such a straightforward question.

Ryan sighs in disappointment and shakes his head. "Let down mate. That is so sad", continues Ryan.

"You're being played mate", casually adds Bill while holding his pint.

"Buying that silly bitch round after round? She won't even let you get your leg over? What do you do round her house?", challengingly puts Robert to Fenton.

"I've never been round her house", regretfully answers Fenton as his face drops in sadness, expecting the incoming flurry of criticism from the lads.

Robert smiles in a nasty way where he appears happy in victory. This information only supports Robert's argument that Fenton is being taken for a mug.

"Where do you go when you leave the pub with her then?", quickly asks Robert, his spirits heightened by the fact he's closing in on how illegitimate Fenton's relationship with Incendia really is.

"Nowhere. We just hang out", briefly answers Fenton to the animated Robert.

"Where you been all this time then?", curiously asks Spiker.

"We were laying down on the pavement watching the stars", painfully declares Fenton in his foolish honesty. His answer is met by hysterical laughing from the lads.

"Didn't you think to do her on the pavement?", mockingly asks Ryan.

"No", answers Fenton like a prisoner in a war camp, answering questions he's reluctant to answer, but feels he as to answer them anyway.

"Not a blowjob or nothing?", rudely asks Spiker. Fenton doesn't bother to answer that question. He just nods his head left to right to indicate that the answer is 'no'.

Spiker grabs Fenton's fingers and sniffs them. "Didn't you even get a feel up?", Spiker jokes. Fenton looks mortified, but the lads just surround him and laugh.

"Look at him, he looks gutted. I would be too if I spent all that money on a bird for piss all", cruelly taunts Robert.

Ryan taps Fenton on the back and reassures him with, "Here now, here now, don't take it personally mate. We just say it how it is. Don't we lads?".

"Too right mate", comes out from Bill.

"We're looking out for you mate. You've had your fun and thrown enough money away on that brass. It's time to stop mugging yourself off", demands Robert. Fenton only returns a distasteful look to Robert, unwilling to listen.

"What the fuck do you want to go out with her for anyway? She dresses like a satan worshipper? That sick shit gets you off does it?", criticises Bill. Fenton just stands there looking offended, resistantly remaining silent.

"Honestly, Fenton, she comes in here every weekend tarted up, talking to a different bloke each night. She always aims for the sad, sorry, numb looking loner like you, no offence mate. Every dopey fucking clown buys her round after round. It's all a game to her. She's marking you as easy prey. Don't let her humiliate yourself Fenton. Stand up for yourself here!", is the advice Spiker gives to Fenton.

"It's true mate, we're not making this up. She has a different bloke on the hook every week, they're all so thick that they think they're in with her. Not one of them gets to go home and fuck her. Whatever you do, do not, I mean do not, buy that fucking cow a drink. She's pure evil!", enforces Bill while holding his pint.

"That ain't all. Tell him Robert", insists Ryan.

"No...I don't want to tell him that superstitious shit. He wouldn't believe me anyway", blurts out Robert, comfortably sat by the bar.

"No, you gotta tell him Robert. He has a right to know", continues Ryan.

Robert pauses for a moment and looks at Fenton, takes a swig from his pint, looks down for a moment as if he is deep in thought, then comes out with, "Alright then, I'll tell him". Fenton can't figure out if this all a performance by Robert.

"That pentagram round her neck ain't no fucking accessory my son! It's a symbol of her religion. Her roots are linked to a family of witches. There are myths about how the locals used to hang her ancestors with rope on the trees at the top of Harrow Hill. These witches, they seduce blokes and put a spell on them, trapping them into an eternity of suffering. They become tramped in a nightmare world. Legend has it that the spell requires the seed of the fella for the witch to cast the spell. Those that cum in the witch are handing their soul to her. It's like handing over the keys to your spirit over to a demon. If ya don't believe me, ask the lads here, they'll tell ya", is the tale Robert tells to Fenton and the lads.

"He's not taking the piss. Remember Tom Maguire? He dated Incendia before he got locked up in the nut house. In fact, it was just after he started buying her drinks in here that he started hallucinating and going nuts. The lad kept saying he could hear voices and see ghouls. He's still locked up in the wards now, his parents were devastated over it", tells Spiker.

"Who was that other bloke that killed himself over her?", says Bill.

"That was that Shane Flannagan. He was in here buying that bitch round after round all night while smiling about it too. She dumped him one day and he came in here to find her drinking round a table with three blokes she just met. The lad was so heart broken that he went to a pub up the road there and drank himself silly. The staff found him dead in the gents' toilets, the poor fucker slashed his own wrists and bled out while sitting on the toilet seat. All the while, that fucking slag denies anything to do with it", explains Robert.

"She's a twisted little bitch Fenton, I'd have fuck all to do with her if I was you", says Spiker.

Robert points directly at Fenton and loudly says, "You, mate, need to fuck up! Get your act together. Don't be coming here to meet that rotten bitch again".

Fenton looks miserable and is lost for words. Ryan escorts him out the pub where the two have a long debate as they walk to Harrow on the Hill station. Fenton expresses how frustrated at how rude the lads are to him, how he thinks no one is happy for him to be in a relationship. Finally, the two arrive at the bottom of the hill.

"Listen buddy, I know the lads can be tough, but it's tough love. They've known Incendia for years. They have your interests at heart. That witch shite is probably made up by Robert, but it's true about those lads going mad after dating her. She's dangerous like, really dangerous. You've pulled – you made it. Don't go any further or you'll end up losing the plot", explains Ryan.

"Alright man, I won't", says Fenton.

"Promise me? I'm looking out for you here. Promise me you won't link up with that devil doll ever again?", asks Ryan.

Fenton sighs in frustration and lies with, "I promise I won't see her again".

Ryan gives him a hug and says, "That's my boy. Next weekend we'll find you a proper bird. None of that goth shite!".

Fenton stops hugging Ryan and says goodbye. While he walks up the concrete stairs to the entrance of Harrow Hill tube station, Fenton looks back and just about makes out Ryan cross traffic lights in the distance behind him.

Sitting on the tube train home, Fenton looks out the window. Hundreds of lights are visible lit up for miles from buildings and blocks far off in West London. Fenton laughs to himself as he replays the tales Robert told him in his head. He laughs in his own thoughts as to how stupid the idea of Incendia being a witch is.

Fenton arrives to the conclusion that the lads a rotten jealous of him. They can't stand to see him with a sexy gothic bird they probably wank off to every night. He figures even Ryan must be raw jealous of him to have him try and steer him away from seeing her. Fenton smiled to himself on the train ride home. He won, Fenton thought to himself. He was with the sexiest and most tasteful woman ever. It was preposterous to even conceive of not seeing her again. Those lads in the pub with Ryan must think he's so stupid to give her up just because they dish out ridiculous superstitious tales about her being a witch. Fuck those low lives, Fenton thought himself. His thoughts were flooded with daydreams of seeing Incendia again.

A day later it was evening again. Fenton was standing outside Camden Town tube station. The smell of cooking from a portable food stand nearby engulfed the street. Music could be heard from busker playing guitar and singing a few yards away. The streets were packed with all kinds of different people heading out to drink or shop. Floods of people poured out from the many ticket barriers at Camden Town station exit, rubber barrier doors flapping open and shut constantly as people scanned their oyster cards on contactless readers above.

Hitting Fenton like a bucket of ice being poured over him, Incendia's tempting beauty immediately caught his attention as she elegantly stepped through the station barriers. She wore those ferocious steel high heels as usual. This time her hair was straightened out and shiny. Those legs of hers looked smoother too, like she rubbed lotion into them, still wrapped in black fishnet stockings. The most enticing clothing she wore was an all-black PVC leather style skirt, so shiny that you could almost make out a reflection in it, tightly fitted on Incendia. The PVC skirt highlighted her bouncy looking bottom.

Fenton felt corrupted by the skirt already with an underlying urge to grab Incendia's backside. Tucked into the PVC skirt was a white t-shirt that tightly fitted Incendia. On the middle of the white shirt was a black image of a ram's head that appeared like a shadow stuck to her chest. Fenton admired the devilish dress code, finding it sexy.

Immediately, they hug and kiss. Incendia grabs hold of Fenton's hand and leads him through Camden Town. Keeping hold of Incendia's hand, Fenton feels like he's a twig being dragged down the current of a river as Incendia pulls him from bar to bar.

The two find themselves sitting in the corner of a bar, similar to the layout of O'Conner's in South Harrow. Incendia buys shot after shot of sambuca to down, with Fenton taking one with her each time, too sheepish to do otherwise. Blind drunk already, the pair of them huddle together in the corner of the bar and kiss. Fenton is stroking and gripping those fishnet tights yet again, then relishing the feel of the black PVC skirt Incendia wears. This time he can make out and be intimate with Incendia without the lads laughing at him. Incendia, wrecked from multiple sambuca shots, climbs up over Fenton with her hair hanging over her face. She scratches his chest with her nails as she tenses her fingers in the shape of claws. Fenton runs his hands through her hair before kissing her. Lost in a drunken abyss of disorder, Fenton was on autopilot for the rest of the night.

Incendia would dominantly hold Fenton's hand, leading him from bar to bar. Lost in the crowded streets and crowded pubs, Fenton held onto Incendia's waist like it was a life raft leading him to safety. Everything was just a blur now. Incendia with her white shirt stood like a beacon amongst the darkness of nightlife here. Fenton's eyes were only set on her.

Walking down the busy street, Fenton pushes Incendia against a brick wall and kisses her. She lifts one leg up, arching it round his backside, where he grabs hold of it as they make out.

Everything was distorted to Fenton now, drunk as could be, unquestionably following the devilish goth doll, Incendia. She held his hand all night leading from place to place. Her immaculate petite figure had Fenton's whole attention for the duration of the night, where even as she led him off in the streets, he could only gaze up and down at her attractive figure.

Their final stop for the evening was a bar called Underworld, adjacent to Camden Town underground station. The pair of them queue up to get inside, where Fenton held his arms round her waist squeezing her tight, drunkenly claiming to be in love with her. Incendia and Fenton show their I.D to two massive security guards before finally entering, where they walk down a staircase.

Incendia trips down the first set of stairs where Fenton rushes to her aid, picking her up, carrying her down the rest of the stairs like a fairy tale. He held her legs from underneath with his left arm, while holding her up from her lower back with his right arm. Incendia put her arms over his shoulders, holding onto him, gazing up at him like a princess that's fallen in love with a prince that rescued her. Smiling at up at him, she says, "I'm going to make a man outta you tonight".

Gently, Fenton puts her back down, helping her to balance back on her feet after falling. In no time at all, Incendia treads bouncingly to the bar and orders shots of sambuca.

The deafening sound of a rock metal band playing on a stage, with the music booming through speakers throughout the venue, made it impossible to hear anyone speak. The band had a drummer, bass player, guitarist, and lead singer. All of them had multi-coloured hair that was spiked up, piercings all over their face, crazy tattoos all over their body. They played to an audience that moshed up and down to flashing lights and a smoke machine, spewing out smoke from the sides of the stage. The lead vocalist screamed, "Satan! Satan! Satan! Rise! Rise! Rise!", into a microphone gripped hard in his right hand. Interestingly, behind the band and their instruments on stage, was a giant steel pentagram set piece. After observing the stage for a few moments, Fenton realised the pentagram was strikingly similar to the one that Incendia wore as necklace.

"I see why you wear that pentagram now, it's this band. You're a big fan of the band then?", queries Fenton. Incendia just pulls a face and places her hand over her ear to signal she can't here what he's saying. She pulls him into the crowd below the stage and they jump and down to the metal music for hours. Incendia rocks her head up and down with her hair flying all over the place. She constantly throws herself at Fenton. A little later she wriggles her backside, rubbing her PVC skirt against his crotch, helplessly turning him on. No longer able to control himself, he gropes her all over, dangerously drunk and out of control. Incendia leans in and licks Fenton's neck like a dog, grabs his hand, pulls him towards the ladies' toilets.

The toilets at the Underworld were filthy. The walls were graffiti ridden with the usual promotional stickers for other bands stuck on them too. The mirrors over the sinks looked murky and steamed over. Incendia dragged Fenton into a cubicle where the black wooden door had the lock broken on the inside. The tiled flooring was slippery wet from god only knows what fluids lay there, the black toilet seat and lid were in the same condition as Incendia pushes down the lid. Sitting on the toilet seat, she bends her legs up until she lands her steel high heels on Fenton's shoulders. He grips hold of them with both hands, looking down at Incendia who looks back up at him while biting her lips in lust. Incendia retracts her legs, poses like a model on the toilet sit, luring Fenton with the licking of her lips. She stands up and slides her black PVC skirt off, revealing her naked body with only the fishnet tights left over them, the shirt is taken off by her shortly after. Incendia lets her fishnet stockings drop to the floor, until they're being dragged by her feet across the ground as she still wears those heels.

Fenton is frozen. Incendia undoes his belt and pulls his trousers down, starts licking his penis before he can even grasp what's going on. Trapped in the pleasure, Fenton's eyes roll back as softness of her wet tongue goes to work on him. He strokes her hair and face as it continues. Incendia kisses the tip of it before pulling her head away, leans her upper body over, but keeps her legs perched up straight, extending her backside out.

Totally encapsulated by lust, Fenton sticks it in her right away, admiring her figure that is so elegantly positioned like a deer walking through the woods. The rollercoaster of a ride began with Incendia crying out and groaning with every moment she was getting plugged. Fenton got more and more excited, faster and faster, the same way a washing machine speeds up before it's about to stop spinning altogether. The more Incendia groaned, the more he enjoyed it and fucked her harder. Finally, Fenton was fucking like a machine gun, unable to stop for anything, pushing the black wooden cubicle door behind him back and forth, slamming it over and over as he was having sex with Incendia.

Unable to carry on in the overwhelming euphoria, Fenton exploded into a sticky mess, the same way most dirty movies end. Incendia lets out one loud scream as it comes to an end. Fenton is left gasping for breath, smiling in achievement and joy, for the deed was done. His dreams came true, but his nightmares were just about to begin…

Incendia stands up and laughs wickedly, with an unnatural ecstatic echo to her voice. She turns to look at Fenton with demonic red eyes that shone unnaturally bright. Fenton steps back in fear. She wipes her backside with one of her gothic, bony fingers, then brings it up to her mouth where she licks Fenton's semen, swallowing some of it.

The necklace (the only other thing on her body along with her heels) has the pentagram on it burn a smouldering orange colour like it's fresh out of the steel works. Licking the rest Fenton's cum from her fingers, she says in a demonic voice, like she's possessed by the devil, "Thank you boy!", before hysterically laughing. Then puff! Incendia along with her steel heels and pendant necklace glow bright and evaporate into ashes that steam away. She literally disappeared in a puff of smoke.

Fenton, with this private area hanging out and trousers down, gawks with his mouth wide open in disbelief. Not only was it shocking that he had sex with a woman, but equally as shocking that he'd just witnessed her vanish out of thin air with no plausible explanation. Two things that Fenton thought was not possible just happened.

Completely bewildered, Fenton pulls up his trousers and does his belt back up. He's so anxious by current events that he drops down to his knees and throws up into the toilet bowl. Fenton stands up and collects his thoughts for a moment. This can't be real; he mumbles to himself. Did Incendia spike his drink? Is this all a hallucination?

Fenton worries that he didn't even have sex with Incendia after all. What if he was just imagining it all along? To the point where he's stormed into the lady's toilets alone and worked himself off. Fenton cycles through paranoid thoughts in his drunken condition. He concludes the first thing he should do is leave the ladies toilets before gets in trouble for loitering in them alone.

Rushing back out to the crowds below the stage, Fenton comes to a halt as the eery surroundings of the venue startle him. The band on stage is now wearing black robes as if they were in ceremony. The instruments have moved off stage somewhere, with only the giant steel pentagram behind the band remaining. Fenton surveys the venue to see the crowd of rockers and goths absolutely soaked, some of them pouring liquid all over themselves from a jerry can. Suddenly, the toxic smell of petrol fumes reaches Fenton as he breathes them in, making him cough in reaction to how strong they smell. It was then that Fenton noticed dozens of empty jerry cans scattered all over the floor. It was apparent to him then that the fans of this band had doused themselves in petrol.

"Our mistress, Incendia, has taken the virgin seed and opened the gate to the underworld. In flame and fire shall we join her, for our mistress and goddess of the underworld requires the sacrifice of the flesh for thee to enter. For thy goddess Incendia do I release the flesh", creepily speaks out the lead singer of the metal band, that was only moments ago screeching down a microphone to the loud sounds of drums and guitar. The crowds below stood in awe and worship, like they'd been brainwashed, where they then all murmured out simultaneously, "For thy goddess do we release our flesh".

"Let it be...", freakily announces the lead vocalist dressed in his dark robe. He then lifts out a zippo lighter and ignites it. Fenton's eyes widen as he notices the lead vocalist holding the lit lighter up in the air, where he puts two and two together, figuring out what's about to happen. "No you crazy cunt! Put it down", screams out Fenton.

The lead vocalist on stage stretches out his fingers until they are flat and aligned together with his palm, thus letting the lighter drop out of his hand as he does this. Before Fenton even sees or hears the lighter drop the ground, he's blinded by erupting orange flames and the sheer heat that could only be described as jumping into a volcano in swimming shorts. The crowds screamed as they were set alight, running into each other while flapping their arms up and down, frantically panicking as they burned. Fenton too was burning away, screaming in agony, waving his arms like a pigeon flapping it's wings to fly away. With only seconds to think, he tries to run out the venue or to a fire extinguisher that might be on the wall. It was useless though as he knocked into other people running around on fire, where one knocked into him so hard that it pushed him onto the ground. Laying there in the petrol fuelled fire, Fenton burnt to death in seconds beside other bodies that dropped to the ground in the fierce flames beside him. The venue called the Underworld burned like hell. Fenton was too busy dying to appreciate the irony.

Chapter 7: The Realm

Waking up in a daze, Fenton opens his eye lids to behold clouds racing in the sky above him. The wind steadily pushed the clouds through the sky in a steady stream. Was this heaven? Fenton wondered. Surely, he was dead, and the clouds were the borders of heaven where he was transported to after his death. The illusion was quickly dispelled when Fenton leaned up and felt the wooden bench was laying on. He was stretched out on a bench beside the church at the top of Harrow Hill. Looking around, he recognised the brick work of the church and gravestones around it. Feeling hungover and like he'd been hit by a truck, Fenton leans forward with his head in his hands, so dizzy he almost throws up. After ten minutes to wake up properly, Fenton leans his head up and looks around.

"Harrow again? What the hell am I doing here? What happened?", quietly says Fenton to himself while alone on the wooden bench. His memory is in pieces where he tries to puzzle what happened last night. It was all blurry to him. The memories of having sex with Incendia in the toilets were crystal clear along with the memory of being set on fire. If that was true, then how was he still alive and without any burn marks? Fenton dismisses the whole night as an hallucination. Someone must have spiked his drink. He thinks that it was too good to be true that an attractive woman like Incendia would have intercourse with him. More worryingly, what happened to her? What if her drink got spiked too? Fenton had to find out if she was alright.

He pulls himself up from the bench and starts walking down Harrow Hill. Reaching into his pockets, Fenton feels nothing at all. His phone and wallet are missing. This leaves him with no way to get back home or contact anyone, including Incendia. He decides to head to South Harrow to find one of the lads in O'Conner's or Ryan. Hopefully, one of them will lend him some money so he can get home.

Walking through Harrow Hill was strange this time. Mist and fog surrounded the area, where it seemed to thicken the further Fenton walked. The mist became so heavy that Fenton could hardly see a couple of meters ahead of him at one point. Gradually, the mist faded slightly, leaving Fenton to see more around him. It was unusually quiet. There should have been another person walking past by now. There was nothing so far though. Fenton was puzzled that not a single car had even driven past him. Where was everyone? The streets seemed devoid of all life. Maybe it was too early in the morning thought Fenton. There was always a car or van driving somewhere, even early hours of the morning. It just didn't make sense to him. Surely, there must be someone around. Where was everyone? While Fenton walked down Harrow Hill, he looked at houses he passed on the way, trying to see any signs of human life. All the homes he passed appeared vacant. They all appeared to be manor-style properties with driveways protected by steel gates. Fenton just figured this neighbourhood was empty because the residents are millionaires abroad or busy at work in an office somewhere.

The relentless mist still lingered in the air. Rustling in hedges and bushes that Fenton walked past left him feeling spooked.

Walking into the high street of South Harrow, Fenton was now filled with fear from head to toe. There was not one person around. Not one car driving by or even one worker serving at checkout in the shops. Every shop had the lights off inside and the shutters down at the entrances, like no one bothered to get up and go to work today. South Harrow was like a ghost town. Fenton pushed himself right up to the window of the chicken shop next to the underground station, holding his hands over his face so he could see through the daylight reflecting off it. It was dark and empty inside. It was the same situation for every single shop Fenton passed, until he reached O'Conner's pub. Fenton was relieved to find the display lights flashing outside with more lights visible as he approached. The comforting feeling of seeing all the ceiling lights on in the bar followed by the multiple flashing buttons of the slot machine in the pub was a god send to Fenton. Finally, signs that there is another human being left in the Harrow.

Pushing the door open, the familiar sight of the lads drinking around a table with pints took all the dread and fear away from Fenton. It was Robert, Ryan, and Spiker all sat there drinking. There was a noticeable concern in their expressions though.

"Hey guys, am I glad to see you. I'm having one hell of a strange time", calls out Fenton. The lads stand up out of their seats and walk over to meet him, appearing shocked to find him here at O'Conner's.

"Fenton…you're here too. Where did you come from?", speedily asks Ryan.

"Did you see anyone else on the way down here?", quickly asks Spiker.

"No…that's what I was about to tell you guys. Everyone…well…everyone else seems to be gone", answers Fenton.

The lads all frown at him in an awkward silence. They look at him with an uncomfortable seriousness. Fenton could feel the vibes among the lads wasn't normal.

"I woke up this morning with my wife missing from my house. I didn't think much of it until I went to get a pint of milk and the newspaper to see everyone else was gone too", explains Robert to Fenton.

"Was on my way to do a shift at work today. No buses coming or cars anywhere. I walked to work instead of waiting at the bus stop all day for a bus that wasn't showing up. Not a single woman or bloke anywhere. My workplace was shut tight. I tried calling everyone until the only person whose phone was working was Roberts", tells Ryan.

"Similar story with me mate", adds Spiker.

Fenton goes pale in fright. Then says, "Who is running this pub then?".

"Nobody. We let ourselves in through the back and turned everything on. Poured ourselves the pints", explains Spiker.

Fenton is quiet and not sure what to say. He looks at he lads waiting for when one of them to burst out laughing. He's hoping they'll tell him this is some kind of prank before giving him a real explanation to what's going on. Waiting there for a moment, Fenton was waiting for the bar staff to come out from the back and return to the bar to serve drinks. No one came though. The laughs and giggles over a prank from the lads never happened.

"Sit down Fenton. You don't look all that great mate. Get comfortable and have a pint", offers Ryan. Fenton sits down with the lads and Ryan pours him a pint of Fosters from a beer tap behind the bar. Fenton downs half of it immediately.

Spiker is huffing and puffing trying to dial numbers on his phone. He tries everything from all the contacts saved to dialling 999.

"Not one fucking number is picking up. Fuck sake", shouts out Spiker, slamming his phone against the table in a temper.

"Maybe it's your phone", suggests Fenton in a bid to be helpful.

"The same with my phone too. No one is picking up", says Robert.

"Mine too", adds Ryan.

Spiker gets up and walks backwards and forwards across the pub in anxiety, yelling out, "What the fucks going on here? I never seen anything like this. There's gotta be one fucker somewhere".

"Didn't you guys get through to anyone else?", asks Fenton.

"Yeah. Bill was here earlier. He's driving out of town to look for other people", explains Ryan.

"Sit back down Spiker. You're acting like a muppet. Take a seat and relax mate", snaps Robert. Just at that moment Robert's phone rings where he answers it. Fenton can hear Bill's voice faintly from Robert's phone as Robert holds up to his ear. Robert answers briefly with, "Uh huh" and "alright mate", then hangs up fast.

"Well. What's he saying then?", eagerly asks Spiker. Robert looks detached from reality for a moment and stares at the wall while taking a massive gulp of beer from his pint glass.

"What the fuck did he say? Christ sake!", impatiently snaps Ryan.

"Fuck all...he found absolutely fuck all. Not one aeroplane in the sky above Heathrow, not a single car, not a single person...fuck all. He's on his way back now", casually says Robert.

Spiker walks over to the slot machine with flashing lights and punches it hard, causing it to rock back and forth before he erupts out with, "I'm not buying this. It's bullshit. This is a fucking reality T.V show set up or something. There's probably cameras recording us. I ain't in the mood to have the mickey taken out of me".

Following that statement, Spiker grabs a bottle of whiskey from the alcohol cabinet behind the bar pours it straight into a rocks glass.

Bill arrives back about an hour later, parking his car outside O'Conner's. The lads turn off all the lights to O'Conner's pub and make sure it's secure before they leave. Robert lets the lads stay round his house as they all decide it's better to stick together while this mystery continues. Fenton would rather go home, but with no people to operate transport, it would take a day to walk back to Camden. He didn't feel comfortable walking that far by himself when he still couldn't figure out what was going on. Back at Robert's house, the lads eat some steak that Robert has cooked for them. They continue to drink alcohol, with Spiker sniffing lines of cocaine already. Bill stands in front of Robert's HD T.V screen trying to find a broadcasting news channel that would give them some information on where everyone has vanished too. Every channel displayed a no service message on the screen. Ryan is still calling contacts on his phone hoping to get in touch with more people. He was left without any answers or connecting phone lines.

"It's hopeless. What are we meant to do now?", says Ryan in frustration.

"Have a drink and we'll sort this out in the morning", suggests Robert.

"I never see anything like this in my life. Where the fuck is everyone? I say we start searching for more people", recommends Spiker.

"It's the same for miles. Nothing on the M25. Not a single motor anywhere", recounts Bill after driving as far as Heathrow earlier.

"C'mon, let's get some tools and have a look in some places. I'm not standing here all night like a fucking melon", goes Spiker. Fenton and the lads grab some tools from Robert's shed in the garden. The lot of them pile into Bill's car as they head into Harrow for answers.

Bill has his hands on the steering wheel, occasionally operating the car radio, still hoping to connect to the rest of humanity. Spiker sits in the passenger seat while holding a hammer. Fenton is squashed in the back seat with Ryan and Robert. The drive is eery and disturbing as the headlights of car light up only an empty road. The streetlights are on yet houses and properties they pass are all dark and vacant looking.

"Stop the car", says Spiker. "Why", asks Robert. "Just do it", goes Spiker.

Bill pulls over and the lads open the doors to the car and climb out. Spiker walks up to a house and tries to open the door.

"Oi Spiker – what ya doing? That's someone's house for Christ sake!", calls out Ryan.

Spiker doesn't listen or care. He smashes the hammer into integrated windows of a front door, smashing them to bits. Then he inserts his hand through the gap in the door where the windowpane is broken, opening the door lock using his hand from the inside. The door is open, and the lads enter with Spiker. They turn on all the lights to the house and enter cautiously, knowing it's someone else's home. All the lads are worried they've just broken into someone's home, apart from Spiker who is bold enough to force entry.

"Hello…is anyone home? We didn't mean to break in. We're just looking for other people", calls out Ryan. His call goes unanswered. The lads explore every room in the house, switching the lights on to each room one by one. The entire house is empty. There's belongings and furniture like an occupied household would usually appear, but no one there.

"Not a single soul. Let's get the fuck outta here", insists Robert. The lads walk down the road and break into another property. Yet again, no one is home. After leaving another property, they pile back in Bill's car and head to Harrow.

The drive to Harrow is eery and spooky with nothing but empty roads ahead. Bill manages to drive them to Harrow in record time. The lads find themselves walking the plaza. They've never seen it empty before. Closed shops and empty streets await them like everywhere else they go.

"Is any shithead here?", yells out Spiker which is answered back only by the echo of his own voice. The lads inspect vacant shops for signs of life only to find nothing.

"Oh fuck this", yells Spiker as he throws a hammer through the window of a clothes shop. The glass shatters to pieces and the shop alarm sounds.

"Calm the fuck down would ya? We don't know what's going on yet and you're already smashing everywhere to bits", struggles to shout out Bill with the shop alarm loudly beeping.

"I'm not hanging around here a moment longer. Everyone back to the house, now", orders Robert. The lads rush back to Robert's house in Bill's car. On the drive back to South Harrow was still no signs of life. It was as if the lads were the last people left on earth.

The lads entered Robert's house through the front door. Bill turns on the light for the lounge and the lads head on through to the kitchen.

"What the fuck is going out there?", abruptly lets out Bill as he faces the kitchen. The lads stop halfway through the lounge and notice something odd in Robert's back garden. There was steam rising from the pool out back where the water glowed a dark red colour. It was visible through the see-through windowpanes of Robert's back door. The lads walk closer to inspect outside. The red glowing water of the pool was just about visible through all the steam rising from it. They moved closer to see that the water was bubbling like a hot spring.

"What the fucks going on with that pool?", asks Ryan. Robert opens the back door, and the lads gather around the pool to inspect this strange phenomenon. The water stops bubbling. Robert leans over the pool and looks down until he sees a disturbing sign of vandalism. A pentagram (identical in shape to pentagram jewellery Incendia wears) was marked in black at the bottom of the pool. Robert points it out to the rest of the lads who then look down to see it for themselves. Fenton gulps as he lays eyes on the pentagram, knowing full well it's the precise one that Incendia wears on her necklace. It suddenly dawns on Fenton that the situation he is in is dire.

"Look at it. Who the hell marked that pentagram on the bottom of your pool?", says Spiker.

"Only knows mate. The pool was fine yesterday. I have no idea what's happening here", Robert says while looking bewildered.

"It's boiling. Why is the water in the pool red? Something isn't right here. We must be being punked or summin'. This must be a reality T.V show prank. I'm not fucking buying this", moans Bill.

"Look at the detail into that marking at the bottom of your pool. It must have taken someone hours to do that. Who did that? How did they do it under water?", queries Ryan.

Robert looks down at the pentagram marking at the bottom of his pool wishing he could figure out how it got there. Fenton looks bug eyed and frightened as the cold truth of the situation seems more possible. Bill seems uneasy and is out of patience. The lads head back inside. They drink beers and do lines of cocaine while discussing the impossible circumstances they've found themselves in.

Bill sits on a stool placed round Robert's kitchen worktop. Ryan and Fenton also seat themselves on a stool. Spiker sniffs a line of cocaine, then leans up straight with wide eyes.

"Ah that's good. Takes the edge right off whatever is going on", says Spiker.

Ryan tries to call numbers from his phone. He can't reach anyone.

"I've never seen anything like this. I still can't get hold of anyone", says Ryan. Fenton gets up and sniffs a line of cocaine, then Ryan follows after, followed shortly by Robert. Sniffing cocaine was the only thing keeping the lads together.

"I'll tell you one thing, I ain't bloody laughing about all this. I when I catch whoever marked that devil looking shit at the bottom of my pool, I'll cave their fucking head in", threatens Robert.

"I'll tell you what, don't that pentagram look familiar", says Ryan on his thoughts over the pool markings.

"Yeah it does. Ain't that the kind of thing that silly goth bitch is into", says Bill while referring to Incendia.

"That's right – that pentagram is the same one that she wears round her neck", concludes Ryan. All the lads turn to Fenton. Unable to hide his thoughts, Fenton appears shaky and nervous.

"Fenton, you seem quiet. Do you know anything about this?", questions Spiker.

"I...I don't know...", cries out Fenton on the brink of bursting out into tears. Robert clues onto the bleak reality that has come to transpire.

"Fenton! Take a deep breath and relax. Breathe lad, breathe in, breathe out, breathe in, breathe out...", instructs Robert to the rattled Fenton. Taking the advice, Fenton breathes slowly for two minutes and manages to calm down.

"What's wrong with him? What's wrong with you Fenton? It's alright lad. Whatever is going on, we're in it together. We got ya back. ya hear?", says Spiker who then walks over to Fenton and taps him on the back.

"Fenton. Look at me", orders Robert. Fenton looks sharp and alert as he pays attention to Robert.

"I want you to be honest, alright mate. I'm not going to get angry or anything like that. There's nothing to hide. We're here to help you. Now I want you to think real hard about Incendia. When was the last time you saw her? What happened when you last spent time with her", demands to know Robert.

Fenton is silent for a moment. Spiker taps him on the back to reassure him he's in safe hands. "If you know something Fenton then you can tell us. Did she do that marking in the pool?", asks Ryan.

After a moments silence Fenton takes a deep breath and tells the lads, "I thought I was on drugs. The memories of last night were so blurry that I thought they were a dream. Incendia pulled me into a toilet and we…we had sex. Then when it was over, she just, well, she just vanished into thin air. It was like she wasn't really there. Then I went outside the toilets and everyone set themselves alight. It was like a gathering of a suicide cult or something. I was burning, I was dying, on fire and dropping to the floor. The whole thing seemed real. Then I woke up this morning on a bench at the top of Harrow Hill. Then I thought, how can it be real?", explains Fenton about the first signs of paranormal activity taking place. Robert lets out a sarcastic laugh. While pointing his finger directly at Fenton, Robert goes, "You…you daft cunt! You absolute soppy, soaking, little cunt".

Before Fenton even has time to blink, Robert's fist slams into his face, knocking him straight off the stool and down onto the floor. The lads rush to Robert and pull him away from Fenton who is now laying on the floor crying his eyes out. Ryan then leans down to Fenton to comfort him, helps him up and seats him on Robert's sofa in the lounge.

Robert struggles to move as Bill and Spiker hold him firmly in place. The veins were visible in Robert's face as he tensed it so hard in anger. With bulging eyes and grinding teeth, Robert roars out, "Fenton, I'll slash your fucking throat, you little bag of shit".

"Calm him down for Christ sake", yells out Ryan while tending to Fenton.

"Robert – what's wrong with ya? You're losing it mate, ya losing the plot. What's gotten into you?", frantically asks Spiker while holding Robert back with Bill.

"He's fucked us! That little wimp has doomed us", says Robert.

Ryan calms Fenton down and gets him on his feet, puts his arm round his shoulder, leads him to confront Robert. Fenton has a black eye already.

"Right mate. You got some explaining to do, you miserable gobshite! Can you tell me why you just decked my good friend here?", demands to know Ryan.

Spiker and Bill let go of Robert, however they stand close to him, wary that he might assault Fenton again. Robert stares down Fenton for a moment, then smugly laughs to himself. Robert then walks over to a cupboard in his kitchen and pulls out a bottle of whiskey, opening it and pouring whiskey into a rocks glass.

"That's your twelve-year aged whiskey. I thought you were saving that for a special occasion?", says Bill.

"Nah mate – there won't be any more occasions after tonight. There will be fuck all!", insists Robert as he sips the whiskey from the rocks glass.

"What's gotten into you?", asks Spiker who is on the brink of losing his temper. Robert pours himself some more whiskey, then carries the rocks glass with him as he walks closer to the lads.

"I'll tell you what's going on, alright. That witch has got us under a spell. That's why there ain't no people anywhere and that thing is at the bottom of my pool. It's a warning mark. That marking on the pool is a threat. Don't you mugs get it? We're marked for sacrifice!", explains Bill.

"Are you telling me that odd looking slag from the pub is responsible for all this?", says Bill.

"She's a witch. A real witch", answers back Robert.

"You're losing your marbles Robert, every fucking one of them. There's no such thing as a witch", yells Spiker.

Robert just laughs and downs some more whiskey, then he points at Fenton and says, "I told you. I warned you! You didn't listen, did ya? You think you know it all. You just had to go and get that little wiener of yours soaked, didn't ya? Now we're all going to pay the price. I hope it was worth it. Was it good was it? Was she a good fuck?", taunts Robert.

"You need to get some sleep mate. Listen to yourself", Ryan tells Robert.

"You've fucked the lot of us, you little shit. I told you, right, to stay away from that twisted bitch. You think I was joking when I told you she was a witch?", shouts out Robert as he throws his rocks glass of whiskey at Fenton. Dodging the rocks glass, Fenton ducks down quickly, and the glass flies across the lounge until hits the wall and smashes to pieces.

Spiker pushes Robert into the corner of the kitchen to keep him back. Meanwhile, Ryan takes Fenton to a spare room upstairs to keep him out of harms way. Bill stands there with his arms folded, not quite sure what to do with himself. Moments later, Spiker manages to calm Robert down.

"It's all over. Finished.", moans Robert.

"I don't know what's going on 'ere, but it ain't magic, is it? You don't honestly believe in that hocus pocus bollocks, do you?", says Spiker to Robert, attempting to talk some sense into him.

"Why else is all this weird shit happening?", smartly replies Robert.

"Look, let's all get some sleep. Tomorrow we'll get in the car and drive. We'll drive until we until we find help. We'll get as far away from here as we can", suggests Bill.

"You lot can nap all you want. I'm staying awake and keeping watch. It's not safe no more. Nowhere is safe", claims Robert. Leaving it at that, Spiker and Bill head upstairs to sleep a spare room with two beds in it. Ryan and Fenton top and tale in Robert's double bed. Downstairs, Robert sits on a stool drinking whiskey and playing music on his phone. He knew what evil awaited the lads…

Chapter 8: Body Count

Fenton opens his eyes as he wakes up. Screaming and yelling is heard from downstairs. Ryan, laying on the other end of the bed, springs up and is awaken from a deep sleep. Daylight beams in through the net curtains in the bedroom. Bill is screaming and yelling like he's having an emotional breakdown. Both Fenton and Ryan immediately jump up out of bed and head downstairs to see what all the fuss is about. Spiker, who presumably just woke up also, walks out the spare room and heads downstairs just behind Ryan and Fenton.

The lads walk into a horrific and unthinkable sight. Bill has his head in his arms, leaning against the wall in the kitchen, crying his eyes out.

Robert's dead body is sat on his sofa in his lounge, barbed wire sewn into his body multiple times. There was so much barbed wire surrounding his body that it was impossible to even touch it without getting cut. The sofa cushions were soaked through with Robert's blood. Barbed wire was going though his throat, eye sockets, and ears. It was difficult to recognize him. Fenton started gagging at the sight of it.

"Uh no, no, no, this can't be true", cries out Spiker with both hands over his head in disbelief before then dropping to his knees and crying out. Spiker cried out so much that anyone would have thought it was him impaled with barbed wire. Ryan has his mouth gawking open in speechlessness. His brain is having difficulties processing the gnarly sight. Fenton, nervous and repulsed about finding Robert's body can no longer hold it. He runs upstairs to the toilet and throws up.

Bill stops crying and has his emotions turn to anger. He runs up and kicks Robert's H.D television, cracking the screen to bits and causing it to drop to the floor. Spiker gets up and recovers from the shock of finding Robert dead. Ryan lets out a few tears. Spiker hugs Ryan to comfort him.

"Look, fucking look", shouts out Bill as he points at the kitchen floor across the lounge. It was the same pentagram marked in the bottom of the pool, only this time it was marked on the kitchen floor from Robert's blood.

Fenton comes back downstairs. Bill immediately grabs hold of him and pushes him against the wall.

"Is this that bitch of yours? Did that evil slag do this? Uh? Did she? TELL ME!", roars out Bill. Fenton is paralyzed in fear as the giant Bill's angry face looks like a boulder about to drop down on him.

"I don't...I dunno man...I dunno...", squirms out Fenton. Spiker pulls Bill off Fenton. It takes a while for the lads to pull themselves together. Then they gather in the kitchen and discuss what to do next.

"How did anyone get in here and do all that so quietly? I didn't hear a scream or yell in the night at all. Did you lot?", enquires Spiker.

"I didn't hear a fucking magpie sing", says Ryan.

"The doors still locked at the front. The back door too. No signs of breaking in or forced entry. Robert wouldn't have gone down without a fight. He would have been loud. None of this makes sense", comments Bill.

"He must be right. It must be dark magic. How else could everyone just disappear like this?", concludes Spiker.

"Let's get the fuck outta this house now. We'll stay in the pub", suggests Bill. The lads leave Robert's house with his mutilated dead body there.

A short walk to O'Conner's pub and the lads still don't see any signs of life. Once inside, they pour themselves some pints. They converse on what to do next.

"Let's just drive. Let's get as far away from this shithole as possible", says Spiker.

"No – we have to find whoever did this to Robert. I'm not going anywhere. I want you lads to stay here. I'm going hunting", states Bill.

"You won't find no one mate! They'll be miles away by now. Keep your bloody phone on so we can call you. You call us if you see anything out of the ordinary", advises Ryan.

Spiker, Fenton, and Ryan discuss how much of a great bloke Robert was over beers. Meanwhile, Bill drives back to his and takes out a shotgun from his garage. It's a gun he's hid there secretly in case he ever needs to use it. The day goes on, Bill drives round Harrow in his car with a shotgun beside him, desperate for revenge.

Driving round and round block after block, Bill loses patience as he finds no one. It's getting late now, and his patience is running out. The sun gently goes down. Bill puts on the headlights to his car as it just starts to get dark. He calls it quits and gives up hunting Robert's killer. Harrow is still a ghost town with not a single human being existent anywhere. On the drive back to South Harrow, there's a long and wide section of the road that is in between two separate cricket fields.

A figure is standing in the middle of the road causing Bill to break the car immediately. He leans in close to his windshield to make sure he's not seeing things. Lit up in the headlights of his car was Incendia, standing on her steel gothic heels, wearing the usual black fishnet tights and torn purple jumper. Her long black hair was hung over her face. She was wielding a long razor-sharp blade, glistening in the headlights from the car, holding it like it was a sword. The weapon looked brutal and unlike anything Bill had ever seen. It was so thin and pointy. There Incendia stood, confronting Bill's car head on, standing still in a freaky stance in the middle of the road.

The first thing that came to Bill's mind was what Robert said. Incendia must be the cause of all the disappearances of everyone, including the death of Robert. Gripping the steering wheel tightly, Bill studied Incendia who stood still like a statue. What was she doing there? Bill couldn't understand it. He wasn't going to waste time asking her. The mathematics was simple! She was the source of all the current problems the lads were facing. With that in mind, Bill accelerates his car towards Incendia.

The twisted Incendia was fearless, holding her position on the road as Bill's car approached at a dangerous speed. Crash – Incendia is swept off her feet as the front of Bill's car knocks her in the air. She rolls across the bonnet and impacts on windshield of Bill's car, cracking it heavily, then launches into the air until she slams down hard onto the concrete road.

Bill reverses his car, stops, then opens the door and steps out. Incendia's body lay on the road with her arms and legs twisted out of place. Her face was scraped and bruised from the impact of being run over. Bill leaned over her with a wry smile on his face, watching her struggle to move as half the bones in her body must have been broken. Coughing up blood onto the pavement as she lay stuck to the road, Incendia groaned and moaned like she was trying to cry out for help. The pentagram pendant she wore on the chain round her neck was hanging out on the road too. Bill leaned in closer to inspect it, realising it's the same pentagram marking as the one that was marked in Robert's house, both in blood and black paint at the bottom of the pool. Now he was convinced that Incendia was behind everything, or at least had something to do with the sinister activity going on.

"You stupid tart! Why do you dress yourself in all that weird shit?", rhetorically asks Robert. He grabs her by her hair and drags her wounded body towards his car. He opens the boot.

"You got a lot of questions to answer. I'd be worried if I was you love, seeing as you're the only woman left in the world with just us lads. Now, you don't give us some bloody answers, you'll wish I hit you harder with my fucking motor", threatens Bill as he chucks Incendia into the boot of his car before slamming the door shut.

Casually as anything, Bill climbs back into his car and drives back towards South Harrow with Incendia locked in the boot of his car. With his right hand, he lifts out his mobile phone and dials Spiker.

"Guess who I just ran into – that cow! Robert must have been right, she's wearing the same markings that was in his pool. Yeah – I'm bringing her back in the boot – yeah, well, I ran her over with the car. Yeah mate, I had to – cool, bringing her back in a few moments. We'll still be able to get a word out of her in a couple of hours", explains Bill into his phone to Spiker.

Just as Bill hangs up the phone, he drives past South Harrow underground station. Suddenly, his headlights start flickering along with the motor stopping and starting. The car radio abruptly starts playing loud music, then switches to letting out a static interference sound. Bill fiddles with the radio to try and turn it off. The car starts accelerating up the road fast, even though Bill hasn't put his foot down in the car. Frantically hitting the breaks of the car, Bill has no luck as the acceleration continues. He tries to steer the car, but the steering wheel fails to control the direction of the car. It was as if it had come loose from the attaching components that connect it. Stuck in the seat of his car as it blasted down the street, Bill's eyes widened in dread as he realised that he had no control over his vehicle at all. If Bill had time to shit his pants, he would have. Before he could even do that, the car swerved left into one of the abandoned off-licence shops, crushing Bill in his seat.

Trapped in-between the driver's seat and bent metal, Bill bled out from his mouth with shattered glass all over him. He was shaking dangerously and could just about move his arms. The boot of his car opens. Bill looks in the rear-view mirror to see Incendia's fishnet covered legs and heels rise out the boot of his car like a scorpion's tail retracting.

Slowly, Bill extends his right arm towards the shotgun on the passenger seat beside him. Incendia walks slowly to the front of the car wielding the thin blade of hers. It's a mystery to Bill how the weapon is suddenly back in her possession, for he left it on the road after running her over. There was no time to think about that, Bill grabbed the shotgun and gently pulled it closer to him.

Incendia walks over to the front of the crashed car and looks in at Bill who is pinned to his seat. She smiles at him. Bill turns to see Incendia who is suddenly transformed beyond recognition. Her skin looks like it's been rotting like a corpse, her eyeballs are wholly white, no pupils visible. She was in a state of decay where her entire flesh was rotted. Bill, hardly able to move a muscle, petrifyingly observed Incendia climb up onto the front of the car and kneel towards him like a stripper giving him a lap dance. Bill aims the shotgun at Incendia, is seconds away from pulling the trigger when that steel blade of hers charges straight down his throat and out the back of his neck. Incendia had swiftly stabbed his head with her cruel shard-like weapon, then pulled it out of his throat, leaving the weapon soaked in his blood. Bill's eyes roll back as he becomes deceased. Incendia, with her rotting skin and deformed looking face takes the shotgun from Bill's dead hands and walks away from the crashed car.

Meanwhile, Spiker, Fenton, and Ryan are waiting for Bill to return with Incendia as hostage. Fenton drinks his pint quietly in eager anticipation of seeing Incendia again. He had so many questions to ask her, not just about all the strange activity that was going on, but what happened between them. Why was she out in the streets alone? Witch or no witch, didn't she care about him? He wondered if she was a victim in the midst of this strange phenomenon too. The lads were convinced she was their ticket back to normality. Fenton knew better though. Whatever was happening was serious. It could well be that the lads are stuck in this dark realm for eternity as Robert suggested. Did Fenton doom the lads to hell by having sex with Incendia? Only one person would know for sure, that was Incendia. Fenton was dying to see her again regardless of the outcome. He needed conclusive answers to all of this.

Ryan and Spiker joke amongst themselves and are in a much lighter mood upon hearing Bill has captured Incendia. Twenty minutes go past, and Bill still hasn't pulled up in front of O'Conner's pub.

"Where the fucking hell is that daft arsehole? He should be here now. It was only a minute drive from South Harrow station", complains Spiker.

The lads feel uneasy and Spiker has had enough of waiting for Bill. The three of them head out the pub and down the empty streets of South Harrow to see if they can find Bill. It only takes them five minutes to walk to the crashed car where they discover Bill's dead body. Ryan was traumatised at the sight of the car crash, staring at it for over ten minutes, not listening to the yelling and screeching from Spiker who absolutely lost the plot to find Bill's body. Fenton sits down on the pavement, then lays down in a ball covering his face with his arms. He wishes he'd wake up from this nightmare. It's hopeless. Fenton knows he's fucked! Fenton knows him and the lads are doomed. Robert was right the whole time. Incendia is a dark magical witch that sleeps with lads as a ceremony. A ceremony that sends men to the underworld.

Ryan, Spiker, and Fenton are back at O'conner's pub. Unable to cope with the loss of both Robert and Bill, the lads drown their sorrows with shots and cocaine. They sniff lines off the bar unit one by one. There's some tears and hugging along with angry outbursts. The session lasts for three hours where they honour Bill and Robert's passing the best they can. Then Spiker clenches his fists, solely bent on revenge and escaping this realm the lads have found themselves trapped in.

"C'mon boys, c'mon, let's go. We're going to sort this shite out now", adamantly states Spiker. Fenton and Ryan follow him to his car that is parked round the block. They all get in while Spiker drives, wearing a flat cap that he pulls out from the glove compartment. It's one in the morning now. Spiker's plan was to search for Incendia block by block. That's exactly what he did – he drove in the car slowly through South Harrow with Ryan and Fenton also keeping a look out for her. They looked out the car windows to look for any signs of her. She must be somewhere.

Finally, after driving out of a street called Dudley Road, Spiker spots Incendia walking down the street. She staggers along the pavement swaying to side, appearing to be intoxicated. Spiker slows the down the car and turns off the headlights.

"Look – there she is. Over there…", announces Spiker. Ryan and Fenton lean up straight from the passenger seats at the back of the car. They look out the window to where Spiker points. It's definitely Incendia with those unmistakable tarty clothes. Fenton's heart races as he sees her. He has a million questions to ask her.

"Let me go to her. Maybe she'll listen to me", urges Fenton. Spiker shuts him down with, "you'll do no such thing. You keep your silly bollocks back. Ryan – make sure he stays out the way".

"Sure thing" says Ryan in confirmation of Spiker's instructions. Fenton sees Spiker put knuckle dusters on both his hands. Spiker drives slowly behind Incendia, stalking her.

"What's she doing? She looks like she's off her tits", says Ryan from observing Incendia who is hardly able to walk straight.

"That's good. We'll catch the little slut while her defence is down", says Spiker. He moves the car slowly up the street, intent on not alerting Incendia that they are following her. They are only yards behind her. Spiker drives slowly up the street until Incendia slips into the entrance of a dark alley in between two houses.

The lads empty out the car quickly and run towards the alley with Spiker leading the pursuit. Fenton notices a sign outside the alley that has 'Jolly's Lane' written on it. The alley called Jolly's Lane was so long that you couldn't see the end of it until you were at the midway point of the path. To the right was a wooden fence separating the lane to the back gardens of terraced houses. The left of the alley was blocked off by a fence made of steel bars where one could see a large cricket field between the gaps.

Incendia walked up the lane swaying from side to side, knocking into the steel fence to the left, then pushing herself away from it. Spiker power walked behind her with Ryan and Fenton a few meters behind.

"Oi", yells out Spiker while charging up the lane with two knuckle dusters on each hand. Incendia doesn't respond as she still appears to be walking through the lane, struggling to balance herself on her heels.

Spiker walks up behind her and throws her against the steel fence to the right. He presses his right arm against her throat, crushing her.

"Right, you freaky slag! We got ya. Now there's a lot of weird mayhem going on round 'ere, we all think you're responsible", speaks out Spiker to Incendia. Fenton walks closer and calls out, "Incendia, it's me. It's Fenton". Ryan grabs him and makes sure he doesn't interfere with Spiker's interrogation. Incendia refuses to answer both Fenton and Spiker. She can hardly open her eyes and just smiles, completely intoxicated.

"Listen, you fucking...slut, devil worshipping, fuck knows what you are, I don't give a fuck! My fuse is about to blow. Tell us what the fucks going on?", threatens Spiker as he crushes Incendia against the steel fence. The pentagram pendant that Incendia wears around her neck dangles over her chest where Spiker sees it. He takes hold of it to see it's the same pentagram marking that was at the bottom of Robert's pool. Incendia, reeking of alcohol, just laughs in Spiker's face.

"Is this a game to you, is it? Two of my mates are dead. That daft pentagram was in Robert's gaff written in blood. Not pointing any fingers, yeah – but it seems like it's got something to do with you, ok. Everyone's vanished apart from you. Start telling me what the fuck you're doing out 'ere before I jump to some dangerous conclusions. At the moment, love, you're giving off the wrong impression", threatens Spiker further.

Incendia giggles like a schoolgirl. She laughs away, then sticks her tongue out at Spiker in a flirtatious way. Having run out of patience, Spiker lays into Incendia like a boxing match on television at the weekend. The knuckle duster on his right-hand slams into her face like a factory robot pressing down on a conveyor belt. He pounds her in the face over, over, and over. Her head is rebounding against the steel bar fence behind, letting off a small ringing, like a desk bell being pressed repeatedly. A steel piercing stud flies onto Fenton's jeans and drops to the floor from where it's been punched off Incendia's face. More piercings are whacked off her face and can be heard landing on the ground nearby.

"No – leave her alone you bastard", shouts out Fenton, still faithful to Incendia. Ryan holds Fenton back as he struggles to intervene in stopping the violence. Spiker pulls his arm back, tenses it hard, punches Incendia so hard it breaks her jaw. Ryan and Fenton hear the sounds of what could only be Incendia's teeth dropping to the ground from where Spiker has knocked them all out.

Still not satisfied with the brutality towards Incendia, Spiker grabs Incendia and throws her to the ground. He kicks, kicks, and kicks her like he's trying to score a goal in a football match. While he's kicking her repeatedly in the ribs, Spiker shouts out between each kick with, "You…fucking…cunt…weirdo…cunt…absolute…fucking …slag…cunt…weird…cunt…demon…goth…cunt…cunt …bitch…cunt…cunt…slut…cunt…slut…ya fucking odd little bitch! You responsible for this? Did you kill Robert and Bill? You…fucking…rotten…minge…cunt…cunt…".

Having battered Incendia senseless, she lay in a ball in the middle of the alley, blood soaking all over her clothes.

"Someone get her a tampon, it looks like she needs one", jokes Spiker as he stands above the blood soaked Incendia. Fenton feels mortified as the girl he was dating only two nights ago was now beaten to a pulp in front of him.

Unexpectedly, Incendia starts to float in the air. Her legs point upwards to the night sky and looked as if something was pulling her up by them. Astonishingly, the lads witnessed the laws of physics defied as she floated upside down in mid-air. Then she let out an unnatural screech of laughter that seemed to echo all around. The same way a helium balloon floats up in the air when you let it go was the same as Incendia suddenly floated up into the night sky. The lads had their heads pointed up in the sky as they looked for Incendia that floated away so high that she couldn't be seen at all anymore.

"Fucking hell", shouts out Spiker. At that exact moment, Spiker suddenly burst into flames without any logical cause. The whole of Jolly's lane was illuminated by the orange fire that covered Spiker. He screamed and roared out for help as he ran towards Spiker and Fenton, waving his arms in the air frantically as he burned. Ryan and Fenton had no choice but to run for their lives. They ran back through Jolly's lane with the living fireball that was Spiker racing behind them.

Sprinting back to the street where Spiker left his car, Ryan and Fenton run further while the orange light of flames from Spiker followed them. The pair of them managed to get far enough from Spiker, who now ran into bushes in a driveway of a house close by, burning alive. His body collapsed in the bushes, burning them along with him. Ryan and Fenton stood next the driveway of house where Spiker was burning away. The lads took a moment to catch their breath. They looked at the ball of fire in front of them and realised Spiker was nothing but ashes. He was dead. Ryan and Fenton struggled to comprehend what just happened with the orange glow of flames in front of them.

Ryan and Fenton run past Spikers car, leaving it there, the doors still open. They ran all the way back to O'Conner's pub in South Harrow. They took comfort in a pint, feeling rather rattled from recent events.

"He was right, Robert was right", murmurs Fenton. "Incendia is a witch. I've doomed us", he continues. Ryan sits opposite him with a pint. In shock at the death of Spiker, Robert, and Bill. Ryan really is speechless.

"This is all my fault", whines Fenton.

"You couldn't have known", reassures Ryan.

"What are we going to do? Do you think she'll kill us too?", brings up Fenton.

"I dunno – tonight we sleep. Tomorrow we go back at get Spiker's car, we just hit the road until we get help", says Ryan.

Both Ryan and Fenton drink pints and play darts. The pair of them lay out on the pub floor and go to sleep. Ryan, however, has a plan. He pretends to sleep and waits until Fenton is snoring. Confident that Fenton is fast asleep, Ryan tip toes out the pub and abandons him. Then he power-walks out of South Harrow. There was no other choice, Ryan tells himself. If Incendia was a witch, then it was Fenton that allowed her magic into his social circle. She was clearly too powerful to be dealt with or stopped. The way Ryan saw it, his only hope was to get far enough from Fenton. Then maybe, just maybe, he might escape Incendia's curse.

Walking through Harrow Hill, there was still no one in sight. Not a car or person anywhere. Finally, a double-decker bus full of people appears. It drives past Ryan. He looks at in awe and checks every detail of it. The sound of an aeroplane flying through the sky is heard. An old lady walking her dog appears to his left, a couple holding hands walks on the other side of the road. Civilisation was back.

Ryan pulled his phone to see dozens of missed calls and messages, a lot of them from his family. His little brother, called James, must have phoned him twenty times. He immediately calls James back, who happens to be in a pub in Harrow.

Walking down the hill past people and cars, Ryan is ecstatic to see he is no longer in the realm he thought he was trapped in. Meeting his little brother outside a pub in Harrow, he hugs him tight.

"Where the fuck were you? Dad's gone to the police and everything. Mum's losing her mind", says James as he stops hugging Ryan.

"Everyone...they vanished. You all vanished. It was just me and the lads. Robert, Bill...Spiker...they're dead James, they're gone...", cries out Ryan.

"What the fuck are you talking about? Dad was with Robert and Spiker yesterday trying to find out where you were?", replies James with a laugh.

"That goth bird from the pub...she killed em", insists Ryan. James only laughs at the answer. His little brother James tells him to calm down, suggesting they go for a drink in central London seeing as Ryan in insistent of getting out of Harrow.

Sitting on the metropolitan line, Ryan has his head slumped in his hands, feeling like he's losing touch with reality. James sits opposite him as the tube train they are on heads into town.

"I don't know what's happening to me James. It was real...it was real...everyone disappeared. Spiker...he was set on fire", explains Ryan. James bursts out laughing in hysterics, and goes, "What drugs have you been taking?".

The tube train stopped at the next station where every passenger walked off the train apart from Ryan and James. The train pulled out from the platform. Looking out the window, Ryan felt uneasy about the packed platform with every passenger emptied onto it.

"Why's everyone got off the train?", says Ryan. James sits opposite laughing.

"What's so fucking funny?", snaps Ryan at the easily amused James who continues to laugh for no reason. Ryan frowns in confusion. Wembley Stadium comes into view from the train window; however, something is wrong. Instead of the steel arc that hangs over Wembley stadium, there was the pentagram, giant, lit up in the sky over Wembley stadium. It was made from white steel like the arc that's supposed to be there. Ryan is shellshocked to see it.

"James…James…look", stutters Ryan as he points at the giant pentagram. James just carries on laughing.

"James…", cries out Ryan.

"You nonce cunt", says James with a sick smile around his face.

"James?", screeches out Ryan who is scared out his wits and not understanding why his little brother just called him a 'nonce cunt'. James crumbles into a pile of sand. Ryan sees his little brother disintegrate into a pile of dust without any cause. Jumping up in terror, Ryan screams at witnessing James fall apart into nothing, runs down the interlinked carriages of the tube train. He's hyperventilating, bumping into railings and bars as he rushes through the empty carriages. Reaching the last carriage, Ryan frantically bangs his hands against the door to the driver's cabin.

"Driver…driver…let me off this train. Stop the bloody train", screams out Ryan. The request was met by the cruel laughing of a witch, the only witch Ryan knows.

"Ah no…no…", cries out Ryan in dread and disbelief. Incendia was driving the train. The lights in the carriages suddenly switch off, leaving the train shrouded in darkness. Ryan legs it back up to the other end of the train that suddenly stops moving.

Hiding behind a seat, Ryan peeks over to see down the carriages. Incendia is making her way up the carriages with that shard weapon of hers in her hand.

Ryan desperately tries to figure out how to escape. He tries to punch the windows open, but only damages his knuckles in the process. The sound of Incendia's footsteps closing in get louder. He takes out a gram of cocaine and sniffs it as much of it as he can.

Incendia is now only meters away, her hair down over her face so you could hardly see it, elegantly walking towards Ryan with that blade in her hand. Ryan, coked up off his skull, tries to negotiate with, "Please, I don't want nothing to do with this. I ain't got any problems with you. I ain't ever said a bad word about ya. I know where Fenton is. I can you lead you to him – you can have him – he's a fucking weirdo. I have fuck all to do with him, fuck...all!".

Incendia gently walks over to Ryan and swings her blade left and right, cutting him to pieces. Blood is splashed in waves all over the train windows. She cuts him limb to limb until he's a pile of guts in the middle of the train carriage floor, looking like a pile of vomit from a drunken commuter late on a Friday night.

The next morning Fenton wakes up alone in O'Conner's pub. He cries his eyes out to see Ryan isn't there. He presumes Incendia got him in the night. Surely, he was next on the list. He was the last lad left.

It wasn't safe in South Harrow anymore. Fenton figured he might stand a chance if he hides somewhere unexpected. He walks over Harrow Hill where everything is still abandoned. Fenton makes his way to Northwick Park hospital across the fields below Harrow Hill. When he arrives there, he is creeped out to see such an enormous building so empty. The hospital is normally full of patients, nurses, and doctors going through the corridors. Fenton walked through the hospital feeling eery. It was a creepy place to be in alone. He explores different floors of the hospital and looks for supplies.

Fenton connects a morphine drip to his arm and walks around the hospital with it attached. He doesn't feel a thing. Not too long now, the sun goes down, leaving the hospital corridors in a frightening darkness. It's extremely scary, but Fenton doesn't want to turn on the lights in case it gives away he's hiding in the hospital. He sits down in the hospital canteen at a table all alone.

Hours go by where Fenton sits in the darkness, looking at empty tables and chairs spaced out in the canteen. He helps himself to some sandwiches in the canteen fridge. He chews the sandwich alone in the darkness. Then he just sits there off his head on different tablets he swallows. He has no idea what tablets he's even taking; he's just using whatever medication he can find in the hopsital. Sitting alone in the hospital canteen, everything starts spinning. Fenton is buzzing out of his mind. Shrouded in the deep darkness, all alone, Fenton stares at the walls and ceiling. He keeps seeing things, like shadows moving around in the dark. The medication he's swallowed must be giving him mild hallucinations.

Drifting off into his own imagination, Fenton almost falls asleep...until an unmistakable echo is heard from the far end of a hospital corridor. It's the sound of a fire exit door being forced open. Fenton leans up with his heat pumping fast in fear. He gasps in fear and his eyes widen where he focuses and stays alert.

A tapping sound is heard louder and louder as footsteps approach. It's the unmistakable sound of heavy high heels as it can only be Incendia walking down the corridor. Fenton fixes his gaze on the canteen entrance. The slender outline of Incendia walks past, that deadly blade in her hand, heading past the canteen and further down the corridor.

Fenton almost feels like shitting himself. Incendia has found him. He decides there's no point hiding anymore. Why would he want to be alone in this realm of hers? This was all silly he thought to himself. They were together just two nights ago. Fenton decides he will confront her.

Walking out into the hospital corridor, hardly able to stand from all the tablets and drugs, Fenton yells out in a croaky voice, "Incendia…it's me. It's Fenton".

There's a silence for a moment. The sound of Incendia's heels tapping the hospital floor grow louder as she walks towards him. Out of the darkness, Incendia appears, wearing her usual heels and fishnet tights. This time she was wearing a tarty nurse dress you'd expect at a fancy-dress party, all white with a red cross marking on the upper part of the dress. She walks elegantly towards Fenton, hair over her face, blade held up in her right hand. The way she walks towards Fenton is sexy and alluring like a model walking on the catwalk.

"Incendia. I dunno what's going here. You're the only girl for me. It don't matter to me if you're a witch. I love all of ya, including your dark magic. We can put everything behind us and work this out", pathetically begs Fenton while standing feebly in the middle of the corridor.

Incendia doesn't acknowledge anything Fenton said to her. Continuing to walk in her trendy pose, she swiftly slices Fenton's throat with the sharp blade of hers, leaving him to drop to the floor, bleeding out. Incendia walks down the hospital corridor leaving bloody footprints in a trail behind her. She walks off into darkness. Fenton lay down in the hospital corridor in a pool of his own blood – dead!

Chapter 9: Gothic Correctness

Fenton wakes up laying down on a bench next to the church on top of Harrow Hill. This is the same bench he woke up on after the night he had intercourse with Incendia. He immediately felt his throat with his hand as he remembered Incendia slicing it open in the hospital. There was no scar or marks on his neck. Fenton was certain he had his throat slashed. Was that just a nightmare?

A group of students walk past Fenton on a path. He's relieved to see other people. Getting off the bench and taking a short walk down the hill, Fenton sees cars and people passing by. Thank the lord, he tells himself. Everything is back to normal. Reaching into his pockets, Fenton still has his wallet and phone missing. If he was alive, perhaps the rest of the lads were too. He proceeded to South Harrow to O'Conner's pub.

After a merry walk to South Harrow, Fenton was in good spirits, over the moon to see humanity back. He had questions that needed to be answered though. What was happening to him?

Walking into O'Conner's pub, it's near empty. Ryan is serving at the bar. Strangely, Ryan has a beard and looks years older.

"Ryan, hey Ryan. You're alive", calls out Fenton. But Ryan was inhospitable with his head down as he stacked pint glasses. He looked furious to see Fenton walking into the pub.

"Ryan man...it's me, Fenton", calls out Fenton to address Ryan.

"I told you to stop coming here. How many times have we gotta tell you that you ain't allowed in here?", moans Ryan. Fenton's face drops in sheer shock and confusion. Pub goers stare at Fenton while sitting with pints in front of them. He feels like a spectacle and incredibly awkward.

"Ryan...what's going on?", asks Fenton.

"This is the last time...GET OUT!", roars out Ryan who looks unhinged and worn out. Fenton stands there with his mouth open in shock. "I just wanted to ask you...", says Fenton in one last attempt to communicate with Ryan.

"Fuck this", shouts out Ryan who storms off to the back of the pub. Determined to interact with Ryan and to get answers, Fenton sits down on a stool at the bar. O'conner's pub is quiet with no music playing. There's hardy a soul in the pub. It's so quiet that Fenton can hear what few people are in there drinking their pints. It's been twenty minutes and Ryan still isn't back. The bar is left unattended. Fenton sighs out of boredom.

A police car pulls up outside the pub, Fenton notices it through the window. Two officers step out the car and enter the pub. What happened next shattered Fenton's hopes entirely...

A tall gothic police officer with piercings and make-up on his face entered the pub wearing a police uniform. He had piercings on his face and black hair that was fairly long. He looked like something out of a Marylin Manson music video.

There she was, Incendia! She walked into the pub wearing her usual heels and fishnet tights. This time she wore a police officer shirt and with a tarty skirt on. It was a legitimate police officer shirt with I.D numbers sewn into the shoulders. She even had a police radio strapped to her skirt. Yet, she still had piercings all over her face. Fenton walks back slowly, about to have a breakdown upon seeing Incendia.

"No…no…you…it can't be…", says Fenton worryingly to Incendia.

Ryan walks out from the back of the pub and yells, "that's him officers. There he is. He knows he's banned".

"Do you want to tell us wants going here, sir", asks Incendia.

"Incendia, you bitch! You absolute filthy slut", screeches out Fenton.

"Who is Incendia?", asks the tall gothic policeman next her.

"That nasty piece of bitch right there. She knows", says Fenton while pointing a finger directly at Incendia.

"Sir, my name isn't Incendia. Calm down – tell us what's going on here", politely negotiates Incendia.

"Bullshit! Why are you doing this to me? What the hell did I ever do to you?", goes Fenton.

"I haven't done anything, sir. We've been called out here today because your unwelcome here by the owners. My name isn't Incendia. I've never met you before", convincingly says Incendia. Fenton laughs to himself and slumps on the bar like he's lost the will to live. He places his hands over his face, takes a deep breath, then stands up to confront Incendia.

"You never met me, no? We never fucked in Underworld a couple of nights ago? Then all this weird shit happened. It's all you, all fucking you, all of this is your realm of torture – slag", shouts out Fenton.

"There's no need for abuse here. If you keep talking to us in this way, then you will be placed under arrest", warns the tall gothic officer standing next to Incendia.

"You ate my cum. You licked my cum off your fingers, you nasty slice of pussy", shouts Fenton.

"I told you officers – he's a lunatic. Every day now he's coming in here with mad stories. Just get him outta here", speaks out Ryan from behind the bar.

Fenton turns to Ryan and says, "Ryan – what the fuck is up with ya? It's me mate. She killed Robert, Bill, and Spiker too. Don't you know who they are?", asks Fenton in desperation.

"I don't know what you're talking about mate! Yesterday you came in talking about aliens, the day before it was zombies. Now you're on about witches and shite. Just stay away from here ya junkie cunt!", says Ryan.

Fenton turns bright red in anger and roars out, "Look at em, look at the fucking state of them. Do they look like police officers? They got fucking metal in their face. That ain't how an officer dresses".

Incendia and the gothic officer handcuff Fenton. The gothic man tells him his rights as he's arrested.

"I see what you're doing. You smart bitch! Now I see this is still your realm. This is all another way to torture me", says Fenton.

Ryan shakes his head and looks away from Fenton who is escorted out of O'Conner's pub. Once outside, Fenton is shoved into the back of the police car.

Incendia sits in the passenger seat of the car while the gothic officer drives. Fenton is handcuffed in the back. Now and again Fenton keeps bursting out into laughter.

"You seem amused. What's so funny about all this?", says the gothic officer.

"She knows", says Fenton, referring to Incendia.

"I don't know you sir, we've never met. I promise you there's no way we had sexual intercourse the other night either", gently says Incendia.

"Bullshit! You're the biggest, most rotten, stinking slut I ever met. Your nasty fucking pussy – it stinks! You killed Spiker. You set him on fire with ya dark magic. Look at what ya did to Robert and Bill…ya tore them apart", says Fenton while handcuffed in the back.

Incendia ignores Fenton. The car pulls over beside a police station where Incendia brings Fenton to a private room with two chairs and a table in the middle. Fenton is sat down with Incendia and the other gothic officer. Another officer enters the room. This time it was a police officer wearing standard uniform, but he had bleached blonde hair and piercings on his face, wearing red lipstick on his lips. Fenton bursts into laughter.

"What's so funny now?", asks Incendia who is sat on a chair on the other side of the table with her legs crossed.

"What's so funny? What's so funny? He is…that guy…that officer wearing lipstick. I never seen a police officer like it. I never seen a police officer like you. Look at the state of you all with that shit in your faces. Police officers don't dress up like that", says Fenton.

"We live in a multicultural society Fenton. It's not some intolerant dictatorship we live in", calmly says Incendia in a professional manner. Fenton laughs away at her answer.

"I'll do a disclosure with you Fenton, we've checked your file. I'm sure you know that you're a paranoid schizophrenic with a history of abuse towards women", continues Incendia.

Fenton is in hysterics as Incendia speaks to him from across the table looking tarty with her long black hair appearing shiny. She looks attractive in her police uniform. Fenton's eyes look like they are going to pop out of his skull as he laughs so hard. His ribs hurt from all the laughing.

"This is ludicrous! This an absolute joke. You look like a prostitute, not an officer. This is a fucking circus", says Fenton.

"Hence the abuse towards women. We've got a clear picture of where we stand Fenton. I'm sure you won't be surprised to know that you'll be sectioned today under the mental health act…", says Incendia before Fenton interrupts her with a laughing fit.

"This is great. This is great. Couldn't make this shit up. I regret touching your rotten fanny, I really do! I don't care if you're a witch. See when I'm out of these handcuffs, I'll rip your fucking heart out", intensely says Fenton as he grinds is teeth in anger. He looks furious at Incendia.

"I think that's it then. Take him away guys", says Incendia. The two gothic male officers escort Fenton to a padded cell, take the handcuffs off him, shut the door.

Fenton bounces around the padded cell like a kid on in a bouncy castle. He whacks his head multiple times against the padded walls. He's throwing himself all over the place until he's exhausted. Curled up in a ball on the floor, Fenton has given up. All hope is drained from him. Hours go by until the door opens to the padded cell.

Incendia walks in wearing a tarty nurse outfit that was green on the sides and white in the middle. She holds a syringe in her right hand.

"Now you're a nurse. Police or nurse? Which one is it?", sarcastically says Fenton. Incendia stabs him in the arm with the syringe and injects him with a potent drug. The effects kick in immediately as Fenton goes floppy and starts drooling. He drops the to the floor.

Determined to fight Incendia, Fenton crawls up to her and clings onto her fishnet tights with his hands. He tries to grip hold of her, but his muscles go too floppy. He's left paralyzed on the floor of the padded cell, drooling, helplessly stuck with his head against Incedia's feet. He just about turns his head to look up at her. The sight was horrifying…

Fenton witnessed Incendia towering over him. She looked so enormous to him, like he was looking from the bottom of a skyscraper. He was unable to move or speak, only able to witness her lingering over him as her face had a nasty grin. She spat on Fenton's face. Being paralyzed from whatever drug she injected him with, all he could do his sit there and take it. She walked out the padded cell and locked the door behind her. Fenton was left unable to move with Incendia's moist spit dripping down his face, uncomfortably irritating him.

Chapter 10: Eternal Prison of Naïve Lads

Fenton woke up to find himself tied onto a steel pallet of some kind. Everything around him was made of a rusty steel fence. He was being lured down by a tall chain, like a crane or something. Before he could even work out where he was, he was in agony as flames below him burned his skin. All Fenton could do was scream as the metal he was tied to burned. Flames scorched him until his skin was cinders. He burned like a 4 oz beef burger on a garden barbecue grill in the summer.

In relentless agony as his skin melts, Fenton hears Incendia's metal heels tapping against the steel floor around him. She's circling him with an iron rod in her hand, the tip glowing orange as it is smouldering hot. She circles him, walking around him while he's tied to the metal he's burning on. Now and again, she stops, prods him hard with the iron rod, impaling him, burning his insides. Incendia walks round him in circles and randomly impales him with the iron rod now and again. Fenton screams, screams, and screams in pain.

Fenton opens his eyes. He isn't on fire anymore. Instead, he's hanging from the neck by rope on a tree branch on the top of Harrow Hill in the woods. It's dark all around with an autumn breeze and leaf's blowing everywhere. He's choking to death, suffocating as he hangs there. Down below in the shadows is Incendia, looking up at him with a smile on her pale face covered in metal piercings. Her long black hair blows in the wind. Fenton is choking to death, but he doesn't die. He hangs of the rope choking and struggling to breath for hours in the chilly wind. It drags on and on, with each minute passing seeming like a year. Incendia doesn't move a muscle, still standing there looking up at him.

Fenton wakes up strapped to a hospital bed. He's heavily sedated and can't move a muscle, yet he can feel everything. Incendia lingers over him wearing her tarty nurse dress, holding her blade in her hand. Slowly, bit by bit, she carves Fenton with her blade, gently slicing him open like he's a cake. The immense pain goes on for hours. He can feel the dampness of his blood leaking out onto the hospital bed that he's strapped onto. He can't even move his mouth to scream. He has no choice but to endure the excruciating pain.

Fenton wakes up screaming. This time he awakes in a concrete prison that looked aged with cracks on the walls. There is a tiny wooden bed mounted into the walls in wooden brackets, no blanket or pillows. A tiny gap in the wall with four small iron bars reveals the outside. The breeze of the night-time autumn wind from the world outside blows into the cell. Fenton leans up and takes a look through the gap. There's trees and a grassy field with lights of neighbourhoods lit up far away.

Moving back down from the open window, Fenton notices a steel door at the entrance of the prison cell. It also had a rectangular see-through gap in the middle. Leaning up close to the gap, Fenton looked out to what was a corridor made of steel and identical steel doors to other prison cells.

Fenton lays down on the wooden bench in his cell. He sat there alone in darkness, shivering from the breeze that blew into his cell from outside. Then he jumped out in fright as he heard screams from the corridor outside. Fenton leaped up and looked through the gap. He could see orange glowing through the gap of a prison cell door a few yards down. It looked like it was burning inside. Smoke plumed down the corridor. The screams went on and on as it sounded like someone was burning alive. Fenton tried to sit down and relax, but the screams went on and on.

Hours later there was a different kind of screaming. Fenton looked out the gap of his cell door again. He witnessed a hospital bed being pushed through the corridor by two zombie-like beings. They were ghoul-like, flesh rotting away, the surface of their skin gone. What looked like a young man was stretched out on the hospital bed, but he was impaled with what looked like a hundred metal blades. Fenton watched in terror as the ghoul like men pushed the bed of the tortured young man through the corridors. Fenton heard him scream until the bed was pushed somewhere out of range of his hearing.

Suddenly, a ghoul like face appeared outside Fenton's prison cell, causing him to jump back from the looking gap.

"Hello little Fenton. 'Bout time you showed up in 'ere", says a familiar voice.

Fenton walks closer the face that looks in at him from the corridor outside. It's rotten and deformed with scars and pale wasted away flesh. The eyes balls were fully white with no pupils. The face smiled at Fenton. Suddenly, Fenton recognised it.

"Robert...is that you", asks Fenton to the ghoul.

"Have to guess do you? Do I really look that shit now!", jokes Robert from the other side of the door.

"You're back...you're here...what are you doing here?", desperately asks Fenton.

"I work here! Even in death I work. Let that be an example to you, ya lazy cunt! I'm the caretaker here…this is the Eternal Prison for Naïve Lads", explains Robert with what little flesh remains on his face almost falling off when he talks.

"I don't understand what the fucks happening. Why do you look like you're dead? I just want to go home", cries out Fenton.

"Sorry lad – you ain't going nowhere. This is Incendia's magical prison. The souls of the naïve lads that she's slept with remain here forever to be tortured, along with their mates. When she came to my gaff to kill me that night, I dropped to my knees and pledged to serve her. It was the only way she'd spare my soul. Now I manage this hell. It was the only way I could save myself", explains Robert.

"You gotta get me out of here Robert", begs Fenton.

"Sorry mate – no can do. I told you to stay away from her, but you didn't listen to me. I gotta look after my own interests now", says Robert.

"You serve Incendia? How could you? She murdered Bill, Spiker, and brainwashed Ryan to forget me", moans Fenton.

"Murdered…nah mate. No one dies in the realm. The rest of the lads are in separate cells further down the corridor, being tortured, forever!", says Robert in a brutal honesty.

Fenton cries his eyes out on the spot. His spirit is broken.

"C'mon fella – cheer up. Have a gram", goes Robertl as he throws a baggy of cocaine through the gap in the cell door to Fenton. Wiping tears away from his cheeks, Fenton opens the bag of cocaine and sniffs it off the concrete floor.

"Feel better fella?", asks Robert.

Fenton stands up smiling with his pupils dilated.

"Yeah, that's a bit better", says Fenton.

The loud slamming of a door his heard from the corridor outside. Robert jumps back from the door. The all too familiar of Incendia's heels tapping the ground was heard once again.

"Open the door", says Incendia's soft feminine voice from the other side of the cell door.

"Yes, my majesty", answers Robert followed by the rustling of keys. The door to Fenton's prison cell opens with Robert holding it open. Incendia is standing on the other side with a syringe in her hand. Immediately, she storms into the cell and stabs Fenton with the syringe, walks back out again. Fenton drops to the floor, drooling from his mouth, unable to move his muscles.

"Have a good trip fella", says Robert from the other side of the cell.

Fenton slips into hallucinations and nightmares, spasming on the cold concrete floor of the prison cell, his eyes rolling back...

Deep into the horrific dreams of terror and hallucinations, Fenton had a vision. It was the church on top of Harrow Hill, surrounded by a clear blue sky. The sun shined like a beacon over the spire of the church. Fenton could feel the warmth of the light. He woke up to screams of lads hours later, lads that were burning in their cells, or being prodded by an iron bar that Incendia stabbed them with.

Robert was in the corridor whistling. Fenton got up and looked out the gap in his cell. There Robert was mopping blood off the metal floor in the narrow corridor.

"Pssst…Robert…", whispers Fenton.

"Oh, 'ello fella – come back round have ya?", goes Robert.

"Yeah. I have…I had a vision", prompts Fenton.

"Oh yeah…what?", curiously asks Robert.

"It was Harrow Hill. The church on top was full of light and warmth", recalls Fenton over the memory of the dream.

"Say fella – where did you wake up after the night you fucked Incendia?", quickly asks Robert.

"On a bench outside the church on Harrow Hill. Twice that's happened to me after being with Incendia", says Fenton.

Robert's facial expression lights up with hope. He thinks for a minute, then says to Fenton, "Of course – the fucking top of the hill. That's where they hung the witches over a hundred years ago. The hill is an energy force that bounds the souls of witches. You wake up there because the power of the hill is catching you from her magic, like a net. Don't you get it lad? The top of the hill is one the place that can protect you from her magic".

"Oh yeah, how do you know?", replies Fenton.

"The hill is calling to you. Every witch has grounds, usually holy places, that renders their magic absolute fuck all", carries on Robert.

Fenton walks up to the cell door and looks through the gap intently and Robert and says, "Robert, let me outta here. Let me run to the hill. I might be able to reverse the magic she has on us. You wouldn't have to mop these floors for eternity. Do you think the power of the church will kill Incendia?".

"I don't know mate – there's a good chance it could. There's no way to know for sure. I don't know if I want to risk my convenient arrangement with Incendia. If she finds out I let you out, then I'll be tortured for eternity like the rest of the lads. She'll lock me up in of these cells", goes Robert.

"Robert – you don't really wanna be mopping up blood for a thousand years. How can you stand here listening to all them lads screaming? What about Ryan, Spiker, and Bill? Aren't they in here being tortured too?", pleas Fenton.

"They're being brutally tortured all day. I throw em a gram of gear in the evenings. That cheers em up", continues Robert.

"You gotta let me try. It's the only way for all of us to get out of here", pleas Fenton further.

"You ain't got a fucking clue if you can stop her magic. No bloody clown knows if it'll work. I guess you're right though lad. Mopping these corridors for eternity will do my fucking nut in too", goes Robert,

Quietly lifting out a bundle of keys, Robert gently unlocks Fenton's cell and opens the door.

"Now you fuck this up lad, I'll personally torture you when you wind up back in 'ere. Don't let us down! Whatever you do, don't get distracted. Head straight to that fucking hilltop. Don't stop for nothing, ya hear?", proposes Robert.

"I hear that mate. I won't let us down", promises Fenton.

"There's a spiral staircase down the end of this corridor. You head all the way down, turn left once your down there, head out the door to the field. The hill isn't too far away. It's across a golf course and a couple of fields. You just keep going. Chop chop you daft cunt! Run for it", quietly says Robert. Fenton fleas down the corridor as quickly as he can.

Rushing down the spiral staircase and out the prison complex, Fenton runs across a grassy field in the dark, rushing as fast as he can.

Moments later Robert is mopping blood off the floor back in the corridor. Incendia comes marching in her demonic heels while holding a smouldering hot iron rod.

"Open it", instructs Incendia to Robert.

"As you wish majesty", says Robert as he pulls out his bundle of keys. Unlocking the door to Fenton's prison cell, he opens it to reveal Fenton is missing. Robert frowns and pretends to act confused.

"Where the fuck has he gone? He was here only a minute ago", comments Robert on the obvious disappearance of Fenton. Incendia has none of it and stabs Robert in the crotch with the iron rod in her hand. Robert screams in agony as he drops to his knees from the pain. Incendia removes the iron rod from his private area.

"Where is he?", screeches out Incendia.

Robert takes a moment to recover from the agony, then looks up at Incendia smiling, tells her, "Gone – he ain't coming back either. He's going to reverse your hocus pocus bollocks and stop all your shit. You psychotic slag!".

Incendia digs her nails hard into Robert's head and keeps her hand steady. Robert suddenly erupts into flames and screams as he burns away. Incendia keeps her hand on his head, using her magic to keep him burning. He looks like a bright orange flare, lighting up the whole damp metal corridor of the prison complex.

Chapter 11: Crazy Golf

Walking onto the hilly golf course, Fenton treads on finely cut grass. He walks past sand patches and white golf flags sticking up from holes in the ground. Trees and woodland are at the end of the hill in front of him, standing tall and high against purple clouds and mist. The whole sky was an illuminous purple. The strange purple mist seemed to flow all around and in between the trees.

"Fenton…Fenton…", calls out Incendia as she runs towards him out of nowhere. Her skin is soft and pale like normal again. She runs towards him lightly and innocently. Fenton falls back on the ground in fear. Incendia has caught him. The plan is over. He just lay on the grass in defeat, waiting for Incendia to torture him or slash his throat.

"Fenton, there you are, silly. What happened? Did you fall over?", concerningly asks Incendia as she goes to help him off the ground.

"Get away from me you cow. I'm not playing your games. If you're going to hurt me then just get it over with", shouts out Fenton.

Incendia pulls a sympathetic face. She sweetly helps Fenton up off the ground. She hugs him and says, "I'm not going to hurt you. Why would I do that?".

Fenton steps back and looks away from her. She looks upset.

"You're paranoid again. Fenton, it's me, your girlfriend. You have a mental illness, remember. You should remember that I love you regardless of that", Incendia tells him why putting one hand on his shoulder.

"A mental illness?", asks Fenton.

"That's right. One minute you think I'm an alien, then you think I'm an assassin from Russia. What now?", explains Incendia.

"You're a witch – no matter what I say or do you keep gutting me. You trapped me in this realm of madness", insists Fenton.

"Fenton – listen to yourself. It's me, Incendia. You met me in the pub. Those rotten old men gave you so many drugs that the synapses in your brain don't work anymore. I'm trying to keep you away from them. Do you really think I'm a witch? Listen to yourself. Those miserable men in that pub have brainwashed you. It doesn't matter. You know I love you", soothingly says Incendia to calm Fenton down.

She hugs him tight. He holds her waist and remembers how good it felt to have his arms round her. Incendia holds his hand and leads him to a bench at the top of the golf course.

The whole of London is lit up in the distance. Wembley stadium is lit up with its arc around it. The whole horizon is the lit-up city against the backdrop of purple sky. Incendia and Fenton sit on a wooden bench together holding each other's hands. They look over at each other and smile. Fenton laughs to himself.

"What's funny?", keenly asks Incendia.

"I was convinced you were a witch. Whatever drugs those idiots gave me really kicked in", he says.

"That's why you have to stop taking them. I love you Fenton. I want a future with you. I can't do it with you turning on me every weekend after drugs, accusing me of being an alien or a witch. It's hurtful", emotionally explains Incendia.

"It was so real...I kept dying and waking up. I didn't know what was going on", Fenton tries to explain.

"How's this for real", says Incendia before leaning in and kissing Fenton. The pair of them kiss with London all it up in front of them. Incendia leans in on Fenton who strokes her hair, then strokes her legs wrapped in those fishnet tights of hers. She giggles.

Incendia takes Fenton's hand and leads him down a path through the trees.

"Where are we going?", asks Fenton.

"You'll see", ecstatically answers Incendia as she winks and smiles at him. She leads him down a dark and eery path through the trees until a large pond is visible between gapping in the bushes around it. Incendia steps into the pond and pulls Fenton towards it.

"What are you doing?", abruptly asks Fenton, creeped out by Incendia pulling him towards the creepy pond that was undisturbed in the silence of the night.

"Come in. There might be a sexy surprise for you inside", hints Incendia.

Fenton doesn't feel right about this at all. Everything around him looks spooky. He's still creeped out about everything that's happened with Incendia lately. It all still feels real. He knows he's been intoxicated on drugs. Incendia must be right. Witches don't exist.

Fenton walks into the pond, feeling uncomfortable as his jeans are soaked from it. He walks all the way into it until the water is up to his waist. Incendia leans in on him with her arms round him.

"Now what?", asks Fenton awkwardly standing in the pond in sheer darkness where he could hardly see Incendia's face.

"Now I drown you – silly prick!", calmly says Incendia before pushing Fenton over into the water.

Fenton is gasping and screaming with his head down in the pond, bubbles flowing out his mouth and floating to the surface. Incendia's thin arms hold his head down, making him unable lift his head out of the water. He waves his arms around in the pond splashing water all over the place. He screams underwater as he desperately tries to be free of Incendia's grip. Mustering all his strength, he manages to rise from the water and push Incendia back, knocking all of her into the pond. Launching herself out from the pond water, Incendia's face is all rotten and ghoul like once again. Her skin is rotted away. She's still a witch after all. Fenton has been duped by her once again. He sways out the pond until he's back on the path, then runs for his life. Incendia is laughing loudly while still standing in the creepy pond.

Soaking wet from pond water, Fenton runs up the path and back onto the golf course further down. He sees Harrow Hill and the church lit-up at the top of it. Running across the golf course, he makes it closer to the hill with each step. He spots Incendia close by, holding her blade. He immediately drops and takes cover in patch of yellow sand in the golf course. He lay flat across it to try and hide. Incendia was walking close by.

"Come on out pretty boy. I'll make a kebab out of you", shouts out Incendia.

Fenton stands up tall and proud, shouts out, "Fuck you. I'm tired of running from you".

The ghoul Incendia turns to Fenton with her deformed face of rotten flesh, all scarred. She licks her lips and smiles.

"You naïve lad – just like the rest of them. All the same you mortal men, pulling down your pants to women you barely know, having kids that you can't afford to look after. Smashed in the pubs and sniffing them lines at the weekends. You wonder why I do what I do", taunts Incendia.

"You're pure evil", says Fenton.

"Mortal men are evil. Look at ya with your world war ones and twos. You're a plague", teases Incendia while circling Fenton, pointing her blade in his direction.

"Is that it then? Is that what all this dark magic is about? Revenge against blokes?", yells out Fenton, still drenched from pond water.

"Nah love – this just a hobby. What do you expect a witch of dark magic to do?", teases Incendia.

Fenton runs. He sprints as fast as he can from Incendia. His only hope was to make it to the top of Harrow Hill. He looks back to see if Incendia is running behind. Suddenly, he hears zombie like screeching. Incendia is somehow now in front of him, running towards him with that ghastly blade in her hand. Before he can move out the way, he runs into Incendia, who then swipes him with her blade. It slashes his arm where blood pours out. She runs up behind him and stabs him in the back. He drops to the floor with the blade stuck in him. Incendia walks over and places her steel heel on his back, pulls the blade out from him.

"You really are numb. Can't believe you fell for that tale about you being brainwashed on drugs. I don't even need magic to defeat you mortal blokes. You're all thick as shit", tauntingly says Incendia as she stands over Fenton's bleeding body.

Enough is enough – Fenton rises from the ground, ignoring the pain of being stabbed. He knows he is beyond death in Incendia's realm of dark magic. There was nothing to fear. All he had to do was ignore the pain. He pounds his chest and roars like a Viking warrior off their head on magic mushrooms. He rushes over to Incendia and grabs her by the throat. They wrestle each other on the ground, spin round and round as they roll down the golf course. Fenton leaps up and starts kicking Incendia in the face, but she jumps up from the ground and slashes Fenton again with her blade. He's bleeding again, feels faint as he collapses. In that moment he sees a rake about a yard in front of him. Incendia is approaching behind him and ready to cut him up with her blade. Fenton soldiers up and runs forward, grabs the rake from the ground, swipes Incendia with it. The rake splits in half as it clashes with Incendia's fine blade, but he knocks her to the ground. Fenton grabs her blade off the floor and slashes her multiple times while she lay on the grass.

"Hahaha that's it, harder, harder, hit me harder boy! Hit that G-spot", jokes Incendia as blood floods out her mouth while Fenton slices her up with her own blade. The blade was doing nothing to hurt her. Fenton sprints away down the golf course, throws the blade away as it only slows him down carrying it. He runs off the golf course into some more woodlands. He sprints through a field where the only exit is a wooden gate.

Once through the gate, Fenton runs down narrow path leading to a small wooden bridge. To his horror, Incendia was standing in the middle of the bridge, blood soaked, looking diseased with her rotten flesh.

"C'mon Fenton – pull down your pants. How about another blowjob", teases Incendia as she sticks her tongue out, blood dripping off it.

Fenton sprints to her and the two grapple each other. Incendia bites Fenton's arm several times causing him to scream. He manages to push her off the wooden bridge and into a heap of thorny bushes.

Running out from the path, Fenton sprints across the last field left. Harrow Hill was so close now. He could see the church on top clearly. There was a running track and a tennis court beside him. Fenton found a small lane leading up the hill. Just as he got to the start of the lane, Incendia jumped out from nowhere and pushed him to the ground.

Fenton tries to get up, but Incendia boots him in the face with those heavy metal high heels of hers, nearly knocking him clean out. He rises again, only to be met by a kick in the nuts by Incendia, whose heavy metal shoe was like being smacked in the private parts with a brick. Fenton dropped to the floor in a ball.

"Down boy!", teases Incendia as she circles him, walking like a model with one foot in front of the other. She kicks him repeatedly while his down on the ground with her brutal heels.

"Pathetic – you think you're a man? You're a skinny maggot that would be lucky to have any girl. You really believed I'd get with you?", insultingly says Incendia.

Fenton is a boiler about to explode. He leaps up and punches Incendia in the face dozens of times. Pumped with rage, anger, and raw emotion from how much of a let down his life has been, he channels his feelings into fighting Incendia. The feeling of living with his alcoholic father that only speaks down to him, the feeling of never having a relationship that was real, the feeling of losing his mother, the feeling of being laughed at in the pub by the lads, and the let down of Incendia cursing him with her dark magic, all fuel him to become a demon. He pounds Incendia until even her deformed ghoul-like form looked pretty to what she looked like now. Fenton just doesn't stop hitting her. The manic Fenton pulls her arms and legs until they break. He butchers her. She's no longer conscious. She's a bag of battered meat bleeding out on the ground.

Finally, his anger is vented out. The importance of his task comes back to him. Hardly able to walk, he limps up the lane towards the top of Harrow hill. The lane is long a steep. Fenton is bleeding out from the stab wounds Incendia left. He must hurry before he passes out.

Heading up the hill, he's disturbed by the sound of metal scraping the concrete floor of the lane behind him. It's Incendia, her legs and arms twisted, limping up the lane behind him. He goes as fast as he can, but he's too weak. He drops to the floor a few times. The sound of Incendia's metal heels scrapping the ground get louder and louder as she catches up with him.

Incendia limps up to Fenton and grabs hold of his jeans, pulling them off him. He wriggles out of jeans to escape Incendia's grip, boots her deformed face to knock her back.

Limping up the lane with his jeans now removed and underwear showing, Fenton looks like a toddler trying to crawl across a bedroom, his pale legs showing.

Incendia grips his legs with her sharp black nails, pulls herself up against Fenton, then bites down on his right arse cheek the way a dog lock jaws onto someone. With Incendia's teeth biting into his arse, he screams while crawling on his stomach.

For ten minutes Fenton is crawling up the lane to Harrow Hill with Incendia lock-jawed onto his arse, dragging her along with him as he crawls. He yells and screeches, turning round to try shake her off him. Fenton turns round and punches Incendia in the head, desperately trying to get her off him. The more he punches her head, the harder she bites his arse.

Finally, Fenton makes it to the top of the lane. Incendia decides to stop chewing his arse. She stands up and spits out a chunk of his flesh from his bottom like a teenage girl spitting chewing gum onto the pavement. Smiling with blood running down her face, she walks elegantly in her heels after Fenton, still maintaining that catwalk style composure.

Fenton is limping along in agony wearing just his underwear over his legs, half of it chewed and torn like a dog had just ravaged him. Heading up stone steps towards the church, Incendia walks up behind him slowly.

"Where are you going Fenton? Come back 'ere and give me a kiss", teases Incendia with blood leaking out her mouth. Fenton ignores her and limps up the hill with blood dripping down his legs and out his arse cheek. Incendia walks behind him, those heels making the clinging sound of metal as they tap the pavement.

"You don't honestly think that church will stop me, do you Fenton? Why do you wanna do that? Don't you want to work things out with me?", calls out Incendia behind him.

Fenton continues up the hill slowly with Incendia stalking him from behind.

"You're ridiculous! Out of the thousands of blokes I've cursed over the last one-hundred years, you've got the smallest dick outta all of them", cruelly yells Incendia. Fenton, determined to break her curse carries on up the hill.

Finally, Fenton's made it – Harrow Hill church is directly in front of him. Gravestones all around it, the spire looming overhead, stain glass windows and the brick structure of the church all there. A concrete path between the grass leads to large wooden doors at the church entrance. Both of them are sealed closed. Fenton limps up to the door and desperately tries to push them open. They are locked – Fenton can't get inside the church.

Incendia grips Fenton and slams him against the wooden church doors. She leans in and kisses him. Fenton screams as her teeth bite down hard on his tongue. He drops to his knees with his mouth open, blood pouring out from where his tongue has nearly been chewed off by Incendia. Then she kicks him the chest with one of her metal high heels, winding him.

Helplessly laying on the floor, Fenton can only look up at Incendia, towering over him while smiling with her blood-soaked face.

"You blokes really are a joke! Why don't you get to know a bird for more than a week next time before you stick your sloppy dick in her? Just another worthless bag of meat sitting in the pub accomplishing fuck all", taunts Incendia.

Pulling out her razor-sharp blade, she points it down to Fenton, then starts carving his chest with it while he lay helplessly on the grass outside the church.

He screams and yells like crazy while she twists and turns the blade, carving her pentagram symbol into his chest.

"You belong to me boy! We're going to be together for eternity you and I. How's that for a long-term relationship?", jokes Incendia.

Fenton slowly gets off the ground and manages to grab Incendia by her throat. He squeezes her by the throat hard, trying to throttle her. She just looks back at him laughing away at his attempts to hurt her.

Fenton pushes her to the ground. Thinking quickly, he looks around him. Noticing a gravestone close to one of the stain glass windows of the church, he improvises and manages to solve the problem of not being able to enter it.

Sprinting to the gravestone, Fenton then jumps, using it as a steppingstone by pressing his feet on the top of it and boosting himself towards one of the church windows.

Smash – the stain glass window shatters into hundreds of pieces as Fenton dives through it. He lands onto the concrete floor of the church in a heap of smashed stain glass and a puddle of his own blood.

With the church break-in alarm beeping, Fenton walks between the wooden benches of the church up to the alter. Incendia climbs in through the smashed window into the church in pursuit of Fenton.

Standing there soaked in his blood, slashed to bits, wearing his ripped underwear, Fenton looks at the alter of the church in front of him.

"Fenton", yells out Incendia. He turns round to look at her. She's transformed her skin back to normal where she looks youthful and pretty once more.

"Don't do it Fenton. You need me. Even in all this pain and fighting you're with me. That's better than walking the streets alone, ain't it? That's better than sitting in that run-down flat with your dad who is getting smashed all day, ain't it?", calls out Incendia to the bleeding Fenton.

Turning back to the alter, Fenton thinks for a moment, then turns back at Incendia who smiles sweetly at him.

"Fenton…you lost your virginity because of me. You're a nobody without me – just another a single bloke. At least you can say you got a bird when you're with me", proposes Incendia, smiling with her dark-red lipstick covered lips.

Fenton drops to his knees and puts his hands together. He starts to pray. In that moment Incendia's smile dropped, where she screamed out, "How dare you – you loser low-life cunt!".

Incendia clicks her fingers together, suddenly Fenton erupts into flames. He drops to the floor rolling on the ground covered in fire screaming. Through Buddhist monk style discipline, Fenton gets back on his knees and prays, even though his burning on fire, he prays, prays, prays, and prays to God, ignoring the burning sensation.

Suddenly, light beamed through the stain glass windows. It got brighter and brighter. Incendia started to melt out of the blue. She screamed like a banshee as her flesh melted like acid was poured over her. The whole church was lit blindingly by this strange light that was destroying Incendia. The light ceases to shine any longer, but when it did, Incendia was reduced to a puddle of melted flesh, guts, black painted nails, black hair, all dripping down her two steel high heels that stood absent from her body. The holy force of the church eliminated her.

Two elderly looking priests open the wooden doors to the church. They are in shock as they see Fenton on his knees praying while on fire before he then collapses to the ground.

"Holy Christ!", shouts out of one of the priests. Quickly, one of them grabs a fire extinguisher hanging on the church wall, then carries it over to Fenton. The priest removes the pin from the red fire extinguisher and squeezes down the handles, sprays Fenton all over with it, putting out the flames.

About an hour later emergency vehicles are outside the church and Fenton's burnt body is carried out on a stretcher by paramedics.

Waking up in hospital, Fenton is on a ward being treated for severe burns. He opens his eyes to find himself connected to drips and bandages all over him. Robert and Ryan are beside his bed.

"You did it fella, you did it! You sent that rotten tart to her grave. We've won mate!", says Robert who Fenton can just about make out through his blurry vision. Unable to stay awake, Fenton slips back out of consciousness again on the hospital bed.

Chapter 12: Burn Out

It's late at O'Conner's pub. Spiker, Ryan, Bill, and Robert sit around a table drinking pints. They are all laughing away having a good time.

Fenton walks into the pub wearing trainers, a tracksuit bottom, and hoodie. He wears a hood over his face and looks at the ground so no one can see him properly. Once he's set foot far enough into the pub, he pulls back the hood covering his face to reveal himself…

The whole of O'Conner's pub freezes as everyone notices Fenton's face. A young girl serving behind the bar screams her lungs out upon seeing Fenton. His face was black and deformed from where Incendia burned him to cinders in the church. His face was rottenly deformed, and he looked like charcoal with scars all over. He was bald with no hair on his head. He looked like a Vietnam war veteran that was unlucky enough to get caught in a napalm strike. Unlike other times he healed magically from Incendia's attacks, the wounds from the church fire stuck with him, permanently, ruining all of his skin…for the rest of his life.

"Fenton - our hero, come on over here my son", chants out Spiker as he claps. Ryan, Robert, and Bill also join in clapping. The rest of the pub goers, however, were awkwardly quiet and spooked out to see Fenton who looked like he just crawled out of a microwave. The older lady called Maggie working behind the bar had to take the young girl serving round the back for a moment because she was traumatised from seeing Fenton's deformed face.

Bill shakes Fenton's hand where they then sit down round the table. Spiker places a pint in front of Fenton.

"Here Fenton – drinks on me for the rest of the night", says Spiker while smiling positively.

Robert pats Fenton on the back, says, "I knew you could do it. You saved us from that witch and her realm. Shame about what happened to you though mate. You're just as bald as me now."

"We owe you big time mate", thankfully says Bill to Fenton.

"Another day in Incendia's prison and my bollocks would have fallen off being prodded by that iron rod", says Ryan.

"It's ok guys – I'm glad it's all over. Who would have thought she was actually a witch?", quietly says Fenton to the lads.

"I did bloody tell you mate! You young ones have to learn these things for yourselves", retorts Robert.

"How are you mate? I'm really sorry that you've ended up like this. If there's anything I can do Fenton, anything at all?", offers Spiker.

"Nah – nah – it's cool. I'm doing alright. I'm on the high-rate disability benefits because of my injuries now. They've given me a flat to myself now too. I don't have to live with my drunken dad no more", explains Fenton on his life changing injuries have literally changed his life.

"That's good fella – at least you got some loot for yourself. I'd say get a job, but who the fucks gonna hire ya now?", jokes Robert. The lads laugh along with him including Fenton. Hours go by and everyone in the pub has got used to the deformed Fenton walking around O'Conner's pub. They drink shots until the pubs closed to celebrate being back from Incendia's realm of torture.

It's three in the morning and the lads are back at Robert's house sniffing lines of cocaine off his kitchen worktop. They pass the same rolled up ten-pound note between each other.

"You should have seen all that barbed wire in ya Robert, you looked like a pig hanging from the butchers window", jokes Bill.

"Tell you what lads – I never been in so much pain in my life when Incendia set me on fire in Jolly's Lane. That was unlike anything mate", recounts Spiker.

"You should have you seen yourself flapping your arms in the air, you looked like a right nitty. Hey – at least you still got your skin. Look at poor Fenton over there", jokes Ryan.

Fenton sniffs a line where his pupils appear even more dilated as usual as his eyes are the only clear thing anyone can see on his deformed and scolded face.

Ryan answers his phone to hear his girlfriend on the other end. She's outside Robert's front door. Ryan let's her in and introduces her to Fenton.

"This is Fenton. You seen him last time. I know he's gone through some changes, so you probably don't recognise him. He's a hero – he saved us from the witch Incendia", says Ryan to his red-haired girlfriend. She shakes Fenton's hand reluctantly, feeling uneasy shaking hands with what looks like a monster.

"You should be proud Fenton. Not many people can say they've destroyed a witch", boasts Spiker to Fenton.

"Yeah – it helped on my disability assessment when I told them I got burned destroying an evil witch. Then they said

I was mentally unwell and physically disabled. They gave me my flat right away", explains Fenton.

The night carries on and they all sniff cocaine in celebration of Incendia out of their lives for good.

Ryan, sniffing an enormous line of cocaine with his cute red-haired girlfriend beside him, turns to Fenton with dilated pupils, looking off his kite.

"Fuck me! Look at that face. That's the last thing you want to see off ya head at this time in the morning", jokes Ryan about Fenton's deformed face. Ryan laughs away but the rest of the lads remain quiet out of respect.

"Look at him – someone get him some sunblock next time. He's toasted to shit", jokes Ryan inappropriately.

"Ryan. Stop it", yells out his cute girlfriend.

"It's just a bit of banter. I'm just taking the piss. He don't mind. You don't mind do ya Fenton?", says Ryan way too drunk and coked up.

Fenton just nods his head side to side with a mild smile.

"He looks someone forgot to take him outta the oven", continues Ryan with his inappropriate jokes.

"Remember the fish holding the flamethrower in TimeTrippers2 - Fenton? How is he? Bumped into him lately have you?", continues to joke Ryan.

"Ya know what – I'm gonna head off home guys. It's late now", says Fenton.

"Alright mate. Don't get stopped by the police on your way home…don't play with any fireworks or nothing like that…get yourself a smoke alarm to wear round ya neck…put it on a fucking chain round ya…you need it", jokes Ryan.

Fenton walks out of Robert's in a low mood. The lads and Ryan's girlfriend look at Ryan.

"What? I didn't say nothing out of line, did I?", says the drunken and coked up Ryan.

Walking across Harrow Hill with his hands in his pockets, hood over his face, Fenton heads to his new flat in Wembley. He thinks about his new life with deformed burn injuries that Incendia scarred him with. He can't make heads or tales if his life is better or worse.

Back home in his flat, Fenton looks in the mirror of his bathroom to behold his scorched face and bald head in the reflection. He's hardly recognizable.

Rolling up some weed into a roll-up with tobacco, Fenton makes himself a spliff. He lights it up while hanging his head out the window of his new flat. Smoking weed out the window, Fenton looks over at Harrow Hill in the distance. He can just about make out the church spire with the red light on top of the hill. Smoking until he's buzzing off his nut, Fenton exhales the word, 'Incendia' with smoke from the spliff flowing out from his mouth. Thinking about everything that's happened to him while eyeing the church in the distance, he thinks of Incendia and how she's scarred him on the inside and outside. He knows that he will never love or hate a woman as much as her. The witch left her mark on Fenton. Smoking on his spliff with his deformed head hanging his flat window, he mutters the words, 'Incendia....Incendia...'.

The End

Printed in Great Britain
by Amazon